Ernest Palmer's
Dream
and other stories

EARL MCKENZIE

LMH PUBLISHING LIMITED

Editor: K. Sean Harris
Cover Painting by: Earl McKenzie
Cover Design: Sanya Dockery
Book Design, Layout & Typeset: Sanya Dockery

Published by: LMH Publishing Ltd.
Suite 10-11
Sagicor Industrial Park
7 Norman Road
Kingston C.S.O, Jamaica
Tel: 876-938-0005
Fax: 876-759-8752
Email: lmhbookpublishing@cwjamaica.com
Website: www.lmhpublishing.com

Printed in the U.S.A.   ISBN: 978-976-8245-31-1

NATIONAL LIBRARY OF JAMAICA CATALOGUING-IN-PUBLICATION DATA

McKenzie, Earl

Ernest Palmer's dream and other stories / Earl McKenzie

p. ; cm.

ISBN 978-976-8245-31-1 (pbk)

1. Jamaican fiction 2. Short stories, Jamaican

I. Title

813 dc 23

Dedication

For Trudy

Contents

Ras Baga

As I drove on the highway my car was like an oven in the mid-day sun. It had no air-conditioning or radio, so while I baked I could hear only the labouring and futile hiss of the fan, and the hum of the engine. I surrendered to the heat. During my student days, on a winter's day in Chicago, with the cold piercing my bones, I had resolved that as long as I lived I would never complain about the heat of the island again.

So I relaxed as I followed the highway, and stared at the black asphalt in front of me, and at the unbroken white line. I was going up a gradient with canefields to the right and left of me. I had spent all morning visiting some of the schools I supervised. I glanced at my watch. It was time for lunch.

My wife Dawn was an excellent cook, and she liked to experiment with international dishes. This was only one of the many reasons I considered her a treasure. But from time to time I liked to eat the country food I was used to while growing up, so I often stopped to eat at wayside places. It was also a great way of meeting the local people and hearing their stories.

So I pulled up at the next shop I saw. The red sign on the yellow wall said RUBY'S COOL SHADE GROCERY AND BAR. I parked under the big mango tree that gave the place its name. I stepped out of the car into the hot sun, and tried to decide if I would enter the grocery or the bar. Both seemed empty, so, pulled by my thirst, I headed for the bar. I stepped out of the heat into the cool shade, and sat on one of the stools in front of the counter.

There were the usual bottles of liquor, sodas and energy drinks on the shelves. A white refrigerator hummed in the corner. My eyes fell at once on the very erotic calendar on the wall. It showed a nude white woman sitting on a bed while still wearing her wedding veil and tiara; her eyes showed that she was looking forward to her honeymoon night. After a few drinks, countless men must have fantasized about that picture.

"Service!" I said as I rattled my fingers on the counter.

I heard sounds in the grocery section, and then a buxom, dark-skinned woman entered and stood before me. She wore a blue head-tie and had a dour expression. She eyed me suspiciously, apparently recognizing that I was a stranger.

"Are you Miss Ruby?" I asked.

"Yes," she replied with a voice that was surprisingly soft and feminine.

"I would like something to eat. What do you have?"

From the list of items she rolled off I selected a spice bun, a slice of cheese and a bottle of cold beer. The combination of bun and cheese is an Easter tradition on the island, but I enjoy it all year round. Miss Ruby served me.

"It is very quiet here," I said.

"Yes. Not much happening this time of the week. But you hear the sound systems on weekends. And of course, during election time you hear the loud-speakers going up and down."

"Bless the Idren!" said a man's voice behind me.

I turned to greet the dreadlocked man who had just entered the bar. He wore a tam which was in the Rastafarian colours of green, red and yellow, a green dashiki, brown trousers and sandals. He sat down two stools down from me, and I noticed at once that his right hand was missing.

"What happen Ras Baga?" Miss Ruby greeted him.

"Give thanks, sister, to the ever living, ever faithful."

"What would you like?" Miss Ruby continued.

"Gimme a Nutrament and a pack of crackers."

Miss Ruby took a cold tin of the beverage from the refrigerator, opened it and poured the pink contents into a glass. Then she tore a packet of crackers open. She placed the two items before Ras Baga. "Thank you, sister," he said as he raised the drink to his lips with his left hand and relished a long draught. He popped one of the crackers into his mouth.

I was progressing with my lunch and felt my hunger increasing. So I ordered a ripe banana and a pack of peanuts as well. I was becoming very curious about Ras Baga's missing hand, so after a few minutes I turned to him and said, "Was it an accident? If you don't mind my asking." The flash of his eyes indicated a kaleidoscope of troubling memories and associations. He was silent for a few moments and then he said, "We come here to lose everything, Iyah. We will be lucky if we even manage to save our souls."

He told me his story, speaking mainly in what the linguists call Dread Talk, the language of the Rastafarians, and which is a Jamaican dialect. But since I am not a professor of linguistics – I studied geography and then education – I am unable to reproduce it in an approximation of his actual speech. So I will tell it in English, the language of my education and my profession as an education officer.

He left his all-age school without any marketable skill, and just barely able to sign his name. He wasn't very interested in being educated into the Babylon System, as he called it. But now that he 'aged-up' out of school, he had to find something to do. For a while he was apprenticed to a charcoal burner who worked in the hills. But with the increase in the use of electricity and cooking gas, charcoal was going out of style, except after hurricanes. Business became so bad he started looking for an alternative.

One day, after being turned down at a construction site, he was standing on a bank and looking down into the bushes. He noticed a fallen dry tree on the ground, and he could see the figure of a nude woman emerging from the trunk.

He felt an urge to release the figure from the tree. So he got a machete and went down into the bushes to rescue the woman from neglect and decay. He took the trunk home, and with the help of a chisel and hammer he carved away at it for a few weeks. The figure of a beautiful black woman half-emerged from the trunk. "Try and sell it," advised his grandmother who had raised him. So one day he took it to the park in the nearby town.

A tourist couple admired it and took a photograph of him standing with it beside the fountain. "Take it over to the college," a young woman advised him. "Show it to the art teacher there." So he went over to the college and asked for the art teacher. Some students directed him to the art room. The art tutor was an Englishwoman with lively grey eyes. She gasped with pleasure when she saw the piece, and offered to buy it immediately. He felt sorry parting with it, but it was the most money he had ever earned at one time. His career as a sculptor had begun.

Then he joined the Rastafarian religion. He found that their doctrines resonated with his distrust of all things Babylonian. Furthermore he admired their belief that they should be independent craftsmen and tradesmen, and not wage-slaves to anyone. Even St. Paul in the Bible had a manual trade. The Rastas he saw were mainly broom-makers, potters and woodcarvers. Now that he was a sculptor he felt like one of them.

He dropped the name William Wordsworth Henry and called himself Ras Baga. Then he began a relationship with a young woman named Cynthia Wilson whom he had liked since childhood. He called her Abba and designated her his queen. They rented a small wooden house and began settling down. He carved wood under the almond tree in the yard. Abba cultivated vegetables and made hats and mats which she sold in the market in the nearby town. When the government built a new highway which passed right in front of their house, they saw it as a gift from Jah. He put up a wooden sign at the gate which said THE BAGABBA MUSEUM. Motorists began stopping to look at the carvings in his yard, and he began selling pieces. Some of his customers were tourists, and when they returned to their home countries they told their friends about him. He became used to having visitors who came on the recommendation of friends.

It was mid-morning, the time of his greatest creativity. The sun was shining on the hedge of crotons and flowers that Abba had planted in front of the house. He was carving wood and whistling along with a reggae hit on his transistor radio. He would work intensely until Abba called him for lunch.

"Oi Ras B!" It was Clyde, his neighbour, calling to him from the other side of the hibiscus hedge.

"One love my brother," said Ras Baga, looking up.

Clyde looked sleepy. He was slim, of light-brown complexion, and had short hair. The tail of his beige, long-sleeved shirt was hanging out of his trousers. School children had nicknamed him Question Sign because the shape of the back of his head resembled the punctuation mark.

"Me think you reach work long time," said Ras Baga.

"Work? Dem lay me off me dear sah."

"What you saying?"

"Dem lay off two-thirds of the hotel staff. Dem say tourist arrival down. We can re-apply when the winter season start."

"So what you going to do?"

"Me don't know yet. It hard fi cook fi get work. Life getting harder and harder for poor people in this country. And me have to pay rent and mind three pickney. Is a good thing Evadne still have her little helper job, even if dem pay her with the crumbs that fall from dem table."

"Yuh haffi push hard fe sell yuh skill."

"Easier said than done. You can talk , for you making piles of money. Make me go see if any food inna de house."

"Little more, then. Little more."

A few evenings later, Ras Baga was putting away his carvings and tools in the shed when Abba and their three-year old daughter Sheba, returned from shopping and stood at the gate. Abba's broad face had curved, soft African features, and she wore a long, dark-brown dress and a scarf over her dreadlocks.

A bankra with groceries hung from her right hand. Sheba, also growing locks, walked in front of her, clutching the parcel Abba had given to her to carry so she would feel useful. Ras Baga joined them and together they began walking towards the house.

"A big-shot man named Mr. Henriques came to see me today," reported Ras Baga. "He exports crafts to America and England, and is looking into China and Japan. He bought five pieces from me."

"That is very good. I hope you got what I priced them for."

"More or less. He said he really likes my work and will be coming back. Says he tours the island looking for good work."

"So all we have to do is produce."

Back at the house Abba began preparing Ital vegetarian peas-soup for dinner. Ras Baga lay on the bed and thought about the next day's work. He got some of his best ideas while lying down. From listening to his teachers he had learnt that the blind John Milton composed *Paradise Lost* and dictated it to his daughters mostly while lying down.

Michaelangelo slept at night in his day-clothes so he could get up and start working right away before losing the inspiration. Bach said that when he woke up in the morning he had to be careful not to step on the melodies lying before him on the floor. He himself had come to believe that there was certainly some connection between lying down and inspiration. So he kept a sketchpad at his bedside so he could get up and make sketches when the ideas floated up into his mind.

"Oi Ras B! You ever hear about socialism?" It was a dasheiki-clad Clyde at the hibiscus hedge the following morning.

"Yes," said Ras Baga squinting at the log in his hand. "But I-man not interested in this country's politricks. We want repatriation to Africa."

"Well, is socialism me into now. Socialism is love. It says every man is his brother's keeper. But capitalism says it is every man for himself. It is for dog nyam dog. It is bad for the human character. And it has been sucking our blood for hundreds of years. But socialism is for the small man. It is time for the small axe to cut down the big tree."

"Why you don't get a job?"

"I have a job. My member of parliament got a job for me."

"Then why you not at work?"

"That is the beauty of this job. I don't have to go to work. I am supposed to be sweeping the street and planting flowers. But since my name is on the payroll, all I have to do is collect my cheque every fortnight."

"Sounds like cheating to me."

"What cheating? This is my reparation money. After slavery they paid the planters but not the ex-slaves. Is so my MP tell me. I am now claiming what is mine."

"Interesting reasoning," said Ras Baga, "but tell me something. You don't think that a man should profit from the labour of his own hands?"

"Every business transaction is theft," declared Clyde. "The capitalist win and you lose."

"Even if it is your free choice?"

"Most times choice don't come into it. You need food, clothing and shelter. You have to live."

"Well, I believe that if I create something of value, something new, and give it to the world, I deserve to be rewarded for it."

"Rasta taking over the country!" yelled Clyde.

"Jah Rastafari!" Ras Baga chanted in reply. "Ever living, ever faithful, ever sure!"

A few mornings later Clyde and Evadne appeared at the hibiscus hedge. Clyde wore a white T-shirt and blue jeans. Evadne was still in her dressing gown, and her plaits were sticking out from under her head-tie. Both were dour-faced and scowling.

"Ras B, capitalism strikes again!" said Clyde.

"What happen now?" inquired Ras Baga.

"Evadne's boss fled the country. Took one of the five flights to Miami. Say him running from communism."

"He didn't even pay me my severance money," moaned Evadne. "Fled in the night, like Nicodemus in reverse."

"That is bad," said Ras Baga.

"Is only Clyde's little work we have to depend on now," said Evadne.

"Plant it like a seed," said Ras Baga.

"You can gwaan talk like de Bible," said Evadne. "You think we don't see all dem big pretty car coming to buy from you? You turning a big-shot too!"

"Some can run but dem can't hide," said Clyde ominously. "You just watch we and dem. Equality coming! Power to the people!" He raised a clenched fist into the air, and he and Evadne retreated to their house.

One morning Ras Baga observed as a white Mercedes Benz pulled up in front of his house. A shapely, brown-skinned woman with shoulder-length hair came out. She began walking towards him, looking around at the carvings as she did so. She smiled, revealing beautiful, even teeth.

"Are you Ras Baga?"

"Yes I."

"I am Nicole Taylor. Mr. Henriques showed me some of your work. We want to commission someone to do a piece to be presented to a visiting African head of state. Would you be interested?"

"It would be a great honour to send back something to the Motherland."

They discussed business and Ras Baga agreed to the terms and conditions. Nicole Taylor returned to the car and brought him some sheets of printed paper.

"This is information about the leader and his country," she said. "Read up on them, for this may help to inspire you."

"Thanks," said Ras Baga as he took the papers. She told him she would return from time to time to see how the work was progressing. Then she got into her car and drove away. That evening after dinner Ras Baga listened carefully as Abba read the literature aloud for him.

Ras Baga searched and selected the best block of wood he could find. He chose lignum vitae, the wood of the national flower. This was not an undertaking to be taken lightly, he thought. He needed time to meditate, or to Iditate, as he put it.

That night as he lay in bed, with ideas running through his mind, he decided that he needed to spend time alone in the hills before commencing this project. He needed to purify and prepare himself.

The following day he took a country bus up to his old village. He spoke to the old people whose outlook he would try to represent in wood. He visited the graves of his grandparents, and of some of the older people who had fled to freedom in the hills after the abolition of slavery. Then he wandered alone in the woodlands and listened to the ancient trees.

He bathed in the river. He stood on the hilltop and looked at the sea in the distance, the sea that brought the colonizers, the slave ships, and the pirates. What does this place want me to say? he kept asking himself. After his long day of reflection he boarded the evening bus and returned home.

The following morning he awoke refreshed. After his breakfast he took up his working position under the almond tree. He had some ideas about yabbas, baskets and wings, but he still wasn't sure what form the sculpture would take. He would just let it come out of the wood.

"Every capitalist is the same!" he heard Clyde shout from the hibiscus hedge. "Big or small they are all the same."

"What is it now?" he asked, looking up.

"The landlord give we notice. Me tell him say we don't have any money to pay, and that him is to allow us some time. But him say him can't wait. We have to leave."

"And you don't have any savings? Not even a tenth of yuh pay?"

"Tenth? What tenth? Before you can have a tenth you must have a whole. Dem didn't teach you any arithmetic in school? We don't have anything."

"Your relatives can't help you?"

"Relatives? Which relatives? Dem sucking salt through a wooden spoon just like we. Evadne used to join partner but she couldn't keep it up. Lend me a money, Ras B."

"Boy, me grandmother used to tell me: Never a lender or a borrower be."

"We will pay you back, man."

"How?"

"We going to bounce back one day, yuh know, Dread?"

"If you have anything to sell I will buy it. But since banks don't carve wood, I don't lend money."

"So is so yuh a gwaan wid yuh neighbour! You not going to need help one day, too? Dem should kill every Rasta!"

Clyde turned and walked away.

It was evening. After working all day on the foundations of the new concrete house, Ras Baga and Abba were building on the land they had now bought. The carpenters had just left. Abba was at the market. Sheba was in the house doing her homework. Ras Baga was contemplating the form that was beginning to emerge from the block of wood.

"See de informer deh!" he heard Evadne shout from next door. He looked up and saw Clyde brandishing a machete as he ran down the gradient towards him, his red shirt flying out of his pants, with Evadne in pursuit. In a moment they were at the hibiscus hedge.

"Is you tell the police dat me have gun!" said Clyde.

"Gun? What gun?" replied Ras Baga. "How me fi know if you have gun or not?"

"I hear is a Rasta tell dem. And the description fit you exactly."

"Rasta resemble Rasta. And I-man don't have anything to do with Babylon."

"You are a lying, dirty Rasta!" declared Evadne.

"And a capitalist!" added Clyde. "I see how you gwaan wid me. But we going to nip you in the bud!"

He saw when Clyde burst through the hedge, with Evadne in pursuit. He sprang to his feet, but by that time their hands were on him. They wrestled him to the ground. He felt Evadne holding his right arm to the ground. He saw the raised machete in Clyde's hand. He heard Sheba screaming in the house. Then there was the pain, the blood, the horror and the darkness.

He regained consciousness in the hospital. The nurses and Abba were around him. The Cuban doctor was gentle and very helpful. Nicole Taylor came to see him, and said she wept when she saw it on the news.

But the visit by the African dignitary was imminent, so they decided to buy a completed piece from another sculptor. None of the finished pieces that Abba had showed her was suitable. She would keep in touch with him and give him all the support she could.

Clyde and Evadne were not apprehended by the police. It was rumoured that they escaped from the island with fake documents. He hoped he would never see them again.

"This is one of the most horrible stories I have ever heard!" I said to Ras Baga. He stared into his empty glass and said nothing. I felt like offering him another, but thought that he might regard it as pity and resent it. "So what are you doing now?" I continued.

"I paint with my left hand," he said.

I recalled that one of the famous composers had written a piece for the left hand, specifically for a pianist who had lost his right hand in war.

"I would love to see some of your work," I said.

"My house is about half-a-mile down the road," he replied, pointing west. "It is on the left. Just look out for the paintings."

Miss Ruby cleared the counter and we paid her. The wall of the sun's heat hit Ras Baga and I as we stepped outside. "Blessings my brother," I said as I turned towards my car.

"Bless the I," replied Ras Baga.

I headed for my first school for the afternoon. As soon as I entered the gate of a school I could sense the character and personality of the principal. This compound had trimmed hedges, trees with white-washed bottoms, and gardens alongside the buildings. There was a soft hum of purposeful activity. But even the pleasure of an aesthetically pleasing and well-run school was not enough to lift the cloud of Ras Baga's story from my mind.

I walked to the principal's office and was greeted by a smiling Mrs. Yvonne Lee, a short, light-skinned Afro-Chinese woman who wore rimless spectacles and a white dress. She invited me inside, offered me a seat and asked if I would like some refreshments. I thanked her and she left to make the arrangements. When she returned we began going over the school's recent records.

I updated her on what the Ministry was doing about some of her requests. I also told her about some of our plans for the school and the region. A uniformed female student from the Home Economics Department, in a white cap and apron, brought me a glass of cold guava juice and cookies on a tray. I thanked her and she said a cheery "You're welcome, Sir" and left. Mrs. Lee and I began discussing the school's sports programme, and a very talented female athlete I had noticed at Champs.

Our discussion over, I began walking along the corridor back to my car. I glanced through a window and saw an art class in progress. I stopped to look. There was nothing quite like watching a class of children absorbed in drawing and painting. Their concentrated, enthusiastic abandon to self-expression was not like anything else you see in a school.

Although my name was Paul, and most of my friends called me Pablo, I knew that I was no Pablo Picasso. But the creative process fascinated me. I wondered what it was like to be able to create things like that. My eyes fell on a small boy who sat before his easel, and was applying paint to the paper on the board as if his life depended on it. I hoped he would see better days than Ras Baga did.

After two more schools I set off, with the bonnet of my car pointed in the direction of Kingston. My wife would probably have Chinese food ready for dinner, for the night before I had heard her speculating about

Sichuan cuisine. But I decided that when we sat down to dinner I would not tell my wife and five children the story of Ras Baga; that was not the time and place for such a tragic story. I would wait until the time came when I would feel like committing it to paper. I felt that now was as good a time as any, really.

The next time I was in that area I remembered Ras Baga the moment I passed Miss Ruby's shop. I began looking out for the paintings. I found his house without difficulty, and pulled up at the gate. I came out of the car and began examining the pieces on display. Some were the usual 'airport' art of famous beauty spots, but there were also a few genre scenes of the way of life of his community. Most of all there were the Rastafarian pieces, images of Haile Selassie and Marcus Garvey, ships of the Black Star Line, heads of lions and so on. Some were on canvas, hardboard, and the lids of oil drums.

I went through the gate and saw Ras Baga sitting at his easel sideways, shirtless, and painting with his left hand.

"Oi Ras Baga!" I said, and he turned to me, seemingly a bit startled. It was at that point that I remembered Clyde.

"Oh! Is you!"

"How are things?"

"Babylon still in charge."

"And the family?"

"Doing well, thanks."

"I am dropping by to see how you are doing. And to buy one of your paintings."

"Just look around, I."

The paintings inside were very much like those outside. But a slightly larger one caught my attention immediately. It was a seascape with palm trees and a bit of coastline on the left which resembled the map of the eastern end of the island, but the right showed an ominous storm brewing over the water. Part of the storm cloud resembled the map of West Africa. It was a very dramatic picture with plenty of blue, white and black.

"What is this one called?" I asked.

"The African Reclamation," he replied.

"I would like to buy it," I said.

"Since it is you, I will give you a discount."

We settled on a price.

I wanted this painting for our living room, but I knew that my wife would not like it. Like most people she preferred landscapes, preferably with some sky, trees with low branches and some water. Her birthday was coming up, so I decided to buy her a gift. I chose one of a waterfall – she loves waterfalls – and I felt she would also appreciate the flowers, including Easter lilies, which grew alongside it. She would also like the gallings flying above the water.

I paid Ras Baga and he took the pieces to my car. We put them in the trunk.

"There is a Jamaican proverb that I like," I said to him. "Jah alone knows why he breaks a fowl's wing."

"Leave it to Jah, my brother. Leave it to Jah," said Ras Baga.

I told him I would come again, got into my car and drove off. I knew I would always remember his story. I drove away remembering Bob Marley's line about crucifying the dread. But in interpreting this story I would try hard not to let my imagination run away with me.

Ernest Palmer's Dream

Outsiders who saw Ernest in the village square in the years following his dream, would never suspect that he was once rich and famous. Now he spent most of his time on the piazza of the shop begging rum and cigarettes from the men who frequented the bar. A small man with a long face and bushy hair, he wore mostly khaki shirts and pants with many patches, and he was usually barefooted. Sometimes he would sit for hours with his hand on his jaw and a faraway look in his eyes. He often told people that he believed that something good would happen in his life again, and that another stroke of good fortune was just around the corner. Perhaps he would have another dream.

One day, some years before, he had suddenly woken up to the realization that he was getting on in years, and that he was poor. He wasn't dirt poor. He had a bit of land his grandfather left for him on which he planted a variety of crops including yams, bananas and sweet potatoes. On weekends he earned a little extra as an 'ackee-tree barber', cutting the hair of men in the village with the barbering set his Uncle Ray had brought for him from the States. He earned enough from farming and barbering to contribute something to the running of the family home in which he lived with Aunty Lynne and Uncle

Ray, and Aunty Lynne saved some of the money for him. But his aunt and uncle, who had inherited the house from their parents, were both getting old, and they would pass on the house and land to their own children.

He was the illegitimate child of their deceased brother. His mother, who had been an employee of his grandparents, had died in childbirth, and his grandparents had adopted him. Now that people were noticing his grey hairs and his increasing baldness, he began to worry about the future. He had no children and felt it was unlikely that he would start a family so late. He began yearning after financial security, and he began to think of ways by which he could become rich.

He began doing the kinds of things by which, it seemed to him, he could become wealthy: he bought raffle tickets and went into the town to bet on race horses; he began making plans to buy and sell animals; he thought of renting a wayside spot and setting up a small shop. But he lost money on the gambling, and the first goat he bought to re-sell died overnight; and since people laughed at him when he talked about a little bamboo shop to compete with the big one in the square, he gave up on that idea. At night he turned and tossed in his bed as he tried to figure out a way of making a fortune.

Then one night he had an amazing dream or, as he preferred to call it later, a vision. In the dream he saw a fat, very black woman sitting on the ground beside a taya plant; there was a bond, it seemed, between the woman and the earth on which she sat. The woman wore a head-tie and a long dress of slavery times. He just knew, in the dream, that she was one of his ancestors. She began describing a spot on his piece of land, speaking in a voice that was at once spectral and affectionate, sometimes talking and sometimes chanting: "Three steps from the root of the cotton tree, towards the rising sun. Spanish man buried something there, O! Running from the English people dem. Gone to Cuba, O! Gone like kite." She brushed one palm against the other quickly. "Hoping to come back one day. But never to return, O! Never to return." Ernest woke up and saw the light of dawn coming through the creases of the door and window of his bedroom.

He dressed quickly, took up his digging bill and a crocus bag, and hurried to his field. As the sun rose he measured his three steps from the cotton tree and began digging. About two feet down he came upon the lid of a large earthenware jar. When he opened it he saw that it was full of gold coins. He gave a cry of joy as he filled his palms with the gold pieces. "Thank you mam! Thank you mam!" he said to the woman in his dream. "You set me up for life!"

But he did not want anybody to know about his good fortune. Not yet anyway. He put the coins in the crocus bag and covered the jar with earth so no one would notice it. Then he began walking home, secretly enjoying the thought that no one who saw him would even come close to imagining the nature of the luggage he was carrying. When he got home he put the bag in a basket and hid it under his bed.

Then he began dreaming about what he would do with the money. First of all he would buy the attractive property which the Rev. John Simmonds was selling. The Irish clergyman had retired and was returning home. The property consisted of seven acres of well fruited land; an old two-storey house made of cut-stone, mahogany and zinc; a thriving bee farm which he could continue;

and it had a wide view of the sea. Then he would get married; he felt sure that now that he was rich, women would swarm all over him. He would put any money which was left over in the bank and then relax and enjoy the interest.

But before doing any of these things, there was the problem of converting the gold coins to usable cash. He wondered about the wisdom of putting the bag of coins on a truck, taking it to Kingston, and walking into the first goldsmith's shop he saw. Since he knew nothing about the price of gold, there was the possibility that he could be robbed. After thinking it over for a few days, he decided to confide in Maas Winty, the most informed man in the district.

Maas Winty had travelled to many countries before settling down to his tailoring business in the village. He read books, magazines and newspapers, and never missed a radio newscast. The villagers hailed him as a genius, since some of his patriotic poems had appeared in the paper, and he recited them to appreciative audiences at church and school concerts. A natural leader, he was president of both the PTA and the local branch of the Jamaica Agricultural Society. People called him a 'village lawyer' and went to him with virtually every kind of problem.

Ernest found him sitting in front of his sewing machine with an unfinished pair of trousers across his lap.

"Hoy Maas Ernie, come in!" he called, peering at Ernest over the top of his glasses.

Ernest sat on a stool by the window.

"You been looking very thoughtful these days of late, Maas Ernie. What can I do for you?"

With a few firm and clever questions Maas Winty soon got most of the story out of Ernest. He was like that. He knew how to get the information he wanted out of people, and they always ended up telling him more than they planned. When Ernest was finished, Maas Winty raised his glasses over his eyes, put the pair of trousers aside and stared at Ernest.

"I want to see them," he said.

"I will show you one."

"Go get it."

When Ernest returned with the coin, Maas Winty took it over to the window on his left and examined it in the sunlight.

"Looks real to me," he said as he returned to his seat and handed Ernest the coin. "Is plenty of them?"

"Quite a few."

"Leave it to me," said Maas Winty pushing the cloth under the needle. "I will do what I can."

But there was something which Ernest had not thought about. Maas Winty was a correspondent for a newspaper, and a few days later a news item appeared in the paper announcing a major archaeological find which was also of considerable economic value. A woman brought the paper to Ernest's home, and Aunty Lynne sat on the doorstep, put on her glasses and read the article aloud so that Ernest, who was illiterate, could follow it. The woman then left with the paper.

"And you didn't say a word to us," Aunty Lynne scolded Ernest. "The whole island know before we."

"Mi go to Maas Winty for help. Mi neva go for publicity."

"Where is the money?"

"Mi hide it."

"Robbers going to watch you like hawk now."

A reporter from the newspaper came the following day. He persuaded Ernest to dig up the Spanish jar, and he took a picture of Ernest standing beside it. Ernest also allowed him to take close-up pictures of some of the coins. The story, along with the photographs, appeared on the front page of the paper a few days later. Aunty Lynne went into the town and bought two copies of the paper; she put one clipping in her photograph album and mailed the other to a relative overseas. Ernest found himself a celebrity in the village. As far as anyone could remember, he was the first person from the district to get his picture in the newspaper.

The night after he made it to the front page, the men in Vin's Bar bought him drinks and proposed toasts to him.

A paunchy bus driver in a felt hat grinned at him and said, "Man, you put the village of San Juan on the map!"

"And remember us when you come into your kingdom," said a long faced carpenter who was reputed to be the heaviest drinker in the village. "Buy drinks for all of us when you cash in the money."

A few days later Ernest was alone at the dining table having his lunch. He heard a man's voice calling his name outside the gate.

"Mr. Palmer! Mr. Palmer!"

"Hello!" answered Aunty Lynne from the kitchen.

"Does Mr. Ernest Palmer live here?"

"Yes, you can come."

Ernest went to the door and saw a balding man with a prominent forehead and dreadlocks coming towards the house. The man wore a shirt with patterns that looked like a leopard's skin, and thick leather sandals.

Ernest identified himself.

"I am glad I have found you," said the man. "I am Professor Lewis from the university."

They shook hands. Ernest introduced Aunty Lynne who was standing at the kitchen door, and the professor shook hands with her.

"Take him to the living room," said Aunty Lynne.

Ernest led the way and showed his visitor to a seat.

"Let me finish my lunch, Professor."

"Sure."

After lunch Ernest sat on a chair facing the professor.

"I have been following your story with a lot of interest," said Professor Lewis. "I am interested in a subject known as parapsychology, and I am writing a book on its Jamaican manifestations. I am interested in your dream."

"What about it, sar?"

"There are some people who believe that dreams are just mental waste thrown off by the mind. It is sheer chance, they would argue, if a dream coincides with the location of a Spanish jar."

"Sar, I know only what I experience."

"But there are others who take dreams much more seriously. Among them are those who believe in the existence of a spirit world, and who also believe that spirits in that world can send us information through dreams. It is this view that I am examining."

"So what do you want from me, sar?"

"A detailed description of the dream and how you found the jar. I want every single thing that you can remember."

The professor took rapid notes on a pad as Ernest spoke. Sometimes he stopped Ernest and stretched his recollection with sharp, probing questions. When he felt he had extracted all he could from Ernest, he thanked him and left.

A few days later Ernest had another unexpected visitor. Early one morning, while he was still in bed, he heard a woman's voice calling him from the entrance to the yard. He dressed quickly and went outside. It was Mother Edna, the renowned mystic and healer who practised in a neighbouring district. She beckoned him over to the hibiscus hedge, and they stood looking down into the dark cultivation as they spoke.

"Brother Ernest, I have been wanting to talk to you ever since I heard about the dream. I believe you got a call. I think you are one of us."

"What?"

"Not all persons are conductors linking this world and the other realm. You are a vessel of the spirit. You have a gift."

"I never dream anything like this before."

"This was the first time a message came through. Now you must cultivate it."

"I don't want to be any obeah man."

The sound which came from Mother Edna's throat indicated that she was hurt by the suggestion.

"Mr. Palmer! Don't confuse those who heal with those who destroy."

"So what you think I should do?"

"Join my church and grow."

Ernest said nothing. And without saying anything more, Mother Edna turned and walked out of the yard. Ernest watched her statuesque form as she went up the hill and disappeared into the vegetation. He remained standing by the hedge, and he kept looking at the cultivation until it was broad daylight and he could see the trunks, branches and leaves clearly. But by then his mind had moved from Mother Edna's visit back to the practical problem of securing his treasure.

The police came three days later. One was dark complexioned, stocky and had a paunch; the other was slim and light skinned. When they arrived, Ernest had just washed and dressed, and was about to leave for Vin's Bar to drink with the men. First they asked Ernest to identify himself. Then the bigger one said:

"We come to seize the treasure."

"But is my things," protested Ernest.

"No they are not," said the slim policeman. "According to the law they belong to the government and people of Jamaica. They will be put in a museum and studied by scholars."

Ernest felt dizzy as if he was about to faint.

"Pass everything over," said the big policeman.

Ernest thought of lying, of denying the whole thing, but he remembered the photographs in the newspaper and realized that denial would be futile.

"You want us to search the place?" the thin policeman threatened.

Ernest hauled the bag of money out into the yard. The jar, which he had taken home after the session with the photographer, was beside the copper in which they kept water.

"You carry the jar," said the big policeman to Ernest. "We will carry the money."

The policemen slung the heavy crocus bag between them and began going up the hill. Ernest struggled with the jar behind them; it was dirty and it soiled his clothes.

A crowd was gathered around the jeep to watch the capture of the treasure. Ernest heard their laughter. As the vehicle drove away in the dusk, the situation seemed more dream-like than the vision that had revealed the location of the jar to him. Dejected, and with the eyes of the crowd on him, Ernest set off for Vin's Bar.

"How do we know they are real policemen?" asked the heavy drinking carpenter. "Perhaps crooks dressed as policemen gone with your money, boy."

"I know them," said a man who worked with the Public Works Department, "and they are genuine."

"They could be genuine and still plan to keep the money for themselves," said the carpenter.

"And if what they said is true," said the bus driver, "you have still made a contribution to the country. They should honour you, man. And I will buy you a drink for that."

"I must confess I didn't know about that law when I sent off the article," said Maas Winty who had dragged himself away from his books to have a drink and to discuss the matter. "It was an irresistible news story. But I honestly thought that the news story would have brought you some help. Since then I have looked it up in the trunk of books I have under my bed. According to what they call the 'law of treasure trove', the government has the right to keep the majority of the found treasure. But they should give a portion to the finder. You should press them, man. And if anything take them to court."

"Poor little me against the government and police," said Ernest looking sadly into his rum and water. "Not even your dream belongs to you in this country. My own dream and my own land. And dem take it away. Ah not doing anything. Make dem gwaan."

Every night after that, Ernest went to bed expecting another dream that would lead to the fortune he desired. But he had no such dream. His grey hairs multiplied. He found no way of earning enough money to build a little house on his bit of land. He lost hope and drifted. As the years went by, the dream became, in his consciousness, the single most important event in his life, and all other events were organized around it.

One night, a number of years after the dream, Ernest was not in Vin's bar, and the men, remembering his time of glory, began discussing him.

"Maybe it was the devil that came to him in that dream," said the emaciated looking carpenter. "The devil gave him a false appearance of wealth to set him up, then broke his spirit to mock him."

"That is not it," said an old man in a straw hat. "You know why Ernest come so? Is because him never listen to Mother Edna. She said so herself. If he had followed her he would have had both spirit and wealth. But his mind was so much on the money he missed his real call. The communication was the miracle, not the gold. And you ever hear of a call like that coming twice?"

"You ever put that argument to him?" asked the bus driver.

"I tried a couple of times but he wasn't receptive. His spirit is still weeping over that gold."

At that point Ernest entered the bar and they stopped talking. He sat on a stool and waited. It was his habit to sit quietly all night and listen to the conversations. And he always thanked his benefactors profusely whenever they offered him a drink.

But it wasn't another dream that rescued Ernest. An English lawyer named George Parker who was married to a Jamaican and practising on the island had been following the newspaper reports and came to the conclusion that an injustice had been done to Ernest Palmer. A tall man who wore thick horn-rimmed spectacles, he drove to the village and interviewed Ernest at his home.

He promised he would defend Ernest in court. Ernest complained that he was afraid of courthouse and affirmed, with some pride, that neither he nor any other member of his family had ever been inside one. But Mr. Parker managed to convince him. In the court Parker argued that the treasure was lawfully Ernest's and the court agreed.

Because of its historical value, the Ministry of Culture decided to purchase the treasure from Ernest. Even after paying George Parker his fee, he still had enough money to start building his own little house on his piece of land. He became a lot more loquacious in the bar. And each time he told the story of his day in court, he ended with the traditional words with which stories are ended on the island: "Jack Mandora me no choose none."

On Sylvan Hill

The men in The Waterbird Bar were discussing Busha Brandon's death. Maas Wally, a tightly muscled carpenter with a thin moustache, had just ordered a round of drinks. He sipped his stout, returned the bottle to the counter and said:

"I heard his last words were 'Bury me on top of Sylvan Hill'. He been saying it a long time, and especially since he took down sick. But his wife, Miss Ethel, won't hear a word of it. She is bent on burying him in the family plot in the churchyard. She can't understand why he wants to be buried at such a remote place in the bushes all by himself."

Georgie Gee, a fat man with large eyes who stood beside Maas Wally, rattled the ice-cubes in his glass of rum and ginger and said, "There is no road to the top of that hill. And that hill is as steep as a coconut tree, I tell you."

"But Busha loved that hill," said Maas Wally. "Told me so himself, once. Said he bought the property chiefly for the hill. It was something he wanted to own. He could see it from his home, and he liked the way it rose up in the air, sharp and majestic out of the valley to the mists which sometimes covered the top. You should hear him talk about it. And it was also his escape spot.

He used to go up there by himself, sit on top and look down on the river and the valleys. People would see him coming down from it, like Moses, with a refreshed look on his face. It was his private natural park, as he used to call it."

"I owe Busha plenty," said Cutter, a fair complexioned sawyer, who was at a table playing dominoes with three other men. "The lumber mill dem put we sawyers out a business. If Busha didn't allow me to plant a field at the bottom of Sylvan Hill I don't know how me and mi family woulda manage."

Scrutineer, a gap-toothed bachelor who was an active political organizer, banged a domino card on the table and said, "Even though I didn't agree with his politics, we were friends. We argued until late one night right here in this bar. At the end he quoted a writer whose name I don't remember. He said he didn't agree with a word of what I said, but he would fight to his death to defend my right to say it. And then we shook hands and he bought me a drink. To tell you the truth, I had mi eyes on his pretty daughter, but the Rastaman beat me to it."

The men laughed.

Maas Woody, a basket maker with refined features, sat on a stool in a corner. He said, "Busha gave me permission to cut all the roseapple wood I wanted from off his land. Said he wouldn't charge me, but that I should give a monthly contribution to his church. And I have been doing that for years. I have to bless him each time I see his bus leaving for Kingston with my baskets piled up on top of it."

Uncle Charlie, the oldest man in the bar, had stopped for a drink on his way home from a prayer meeting. He looked at Maas Woody and said, "And Busha loved his church, you know. He donated the organ to the church, and he was the only person allowed to play it on special occasions. And everytime he gave me a ride in his car after church he would say, 'Get in Charlie. You have the furthest to walk'. "

Bimrock, a broad-shouldered young man reputed to be the strongest man in the village, shuffled the domino cards and said, "If I didn't work in his fields, I couldn't survive."

Maas Wally said, "Sylvan Hill was like his personal pyramid to him. I propose that we grant him his wish and take his body up there to be buried. Did you know that he is descended from an abolitionist?"

"A what?" said Bimrock.

"Abolitionist," said Maas Wally. "The people who fought to end slavery."

"His family go far back," said Scrutineer.

"Way back to Scotland. Him tell me the whole story."

"Any man whose forefathers helped to end slavery deserve our support," said Scrutineer. "This is even more reason to bury him on Sylvan Hill. Put my name on the list."

"Me too," said Maas Woody.

"Count me in," said Cutter.

"I must do this for Busha," said Bimrock.

"I am old," said Uncle Charlie, "but I will give it a shot."

"It is the family's business," said Georgie Gee. "Let them bury him where they want."

Maas Wally said, "First thing in the morning we going up there to try and persuade them."

A man in a corner said, "What does it matter where they bury him? When you dead you don't know anything."

"When I die, I want my wishes to be respected," said Maas Wally.

Maas Woody gestured to the bartender for a round of drinks. "Let us drink to Busha," he said. The drinks were served and the men raised their glasses and bottles in tribute. "To Busha!" they said.

The following morning the six men arrived at Busha's home carrying their pickaxes, shovels, machetes and hoes. Miss Ethel, her daughter Cynthia, and her son Frank were sitting on the terrace having breakfast. A maid in a black and white uniform was pouring coffee from a silver coffee pot. The men said good morning to the family.

"We sorry to disturb you so soon, Miss Ethel," said Maas Wally. "We have a matter we would like to discuss with you, but we will wait until you finish your breakfast."

Miss Ethel looked suspiciously at the tools the men had. She was fair-complexioned, broad-faced and wore her hair in a bun. She said, "I don't want you to wait. What is it Mr. Walters?"

Maas Wally explained their mission.

"But it is a family matter, Mr. Walters, and we have already decided."

"I agree it is a family matter," said Maas Wally. "But Busha belongs to the community too, an' we would like to pay him our last respects in this way. And how would you like it if they don't bury you in the churchyard? It won't put you out any. We will do all the work. All you have to do is provide the food."

Miss Ethel looked at her children.

"It doesn't matter to me," said Cynthia, putting marmalade on her toast. She was in her mid-thirties and she had her brown hair in braids. "Let the dead bury their own dead," she said, echoing her Rastafarian boyfriend's dislike of funerals.

"Dem can gwaan for all I care," said Frank, reaching for the stewed guavas. He was older than Cynthia and his straight hair was already receding. A former cricketer, he was now well-known as a drunkard and was in one of his rare periods of sobriety.

Miss Ethel struggled with herself visibly. Then, as if relieving herself of a great burden she had carried for years, she said, "All right. Go ahead and bury him in his bush. It is his land and his wish. But we cannot send food up there for you."

"We will cook our own food," said Maas Wally. "Uncle Charlie here is a first class cook. You just give us what we need."

Miss Ethel called to the maid and told her the items she should give to the men. Then she returned to her sombre mood, obviously still wrestling with the matter. She remained silent while the maid gave the men the food and utensils. Then, as they were about to leave, she relieved herself of some further thoughts: "You cannot lie to God. There should be no unity in a churchyard if there is no unity in life. Let him be."

The men set off downhill towards the gate. Maas Wally stopped and looked across at the view of Sylvan Hill that Busha had seen nearly all his life; it was now blue-green, stately and peaceful, with mist rising out of the valleys around it. The other men passed Maas Wally as he stood in contemplation. As he tried to catch up with them, he remembered the conversation he had with Busha on the terrace one afternoon.

Maas Wally was Busha's carpenter. He was on the roof fixing leaks when Busha called to him and invited him to have a drink with him on the terrace. The terrace was a cosy place with white-painted metal furniture, hanging plants, and lovely views of the surrounding countryside. Busha had a bottle of whiskey, two glasses and a bowl of ice on the table; he invited Maas Wally to help himself. The two men settled down to the liquor, and as the level in the bottle went down, Busha poured his heart out about his disappointment with his family.

After attending one of the most expensive high schools in the island, Frank left unable to do much more than sign his name. Busha bought him a truck and a sound system and set him up in business. He crashed and destroyed the truck in a race with a car and was lucky to have escaped with his life. The sound system made little money, for Frank was not tough-minded enough to collect all his fees from his customers.

When the machine needed a part which was not then available in the island, Frank sold it. After troubles with his girlfriend, the daughter of a small farmer with whom he fathered two children and who had apparently gotten involved with him primarily because of his perceived money and status, he began drinking heavily. The drinking worsened after she began an affair with another man. Busha threw him out of the house and told him to stand on his own two feet like a man. The drinking continued, and when people saw him on the road begging money to buy rum, they shook their heads sadly to think that he was the son of Busha Brandon.

His daughter Cynthia rejected marriage proposals from several prominent professionals and businessmen, and left the family home to live with a Rastafarian in a hut in the bushes. She said she had discovered her African roots. The principal of the local elementary school, a traditionalist and disciplinarian, refused their two children admission to his school on the grounds that with their locks, they were not properly groomed; so they attended a private Afro-centric Rasta school some miles away. Busha himself regarded Rastafarianism as a blasphemous doctrine associated with drugs and crime. His daughter's chosen lifestyle broke his heart.

Then there was his wife Miss Ethel. Busha said he was convinced that she married him, not for love, but for financial security and status. He believed she was still in love with a former rector of their church. He had never seen her look at him the way she looked at that rector. Rumour of the love affair had been all over the community. They transferred the clergyman, but he maintained a friendship with Miss Ethel through correspondence. Busha felt that with Miss Ethel he had the form of a marriage, but it was without a glow of mutual love and compassion at its core.

Busha Brandon then told him about his family history of his early Quaker and Afro-Scottish ancestry, and their role in the abolition movement.

Maas Wally remembered Busha, almost inebriated, slumped in his chair, looking wistfully across the valley at Sylvan Hill. That was the first time Maas Wally heard him express his desire to be buried there. That afternoon Busha had appeared to him as a wealthy but lonely and broken man. And now, as he hurried to catch up with his fellow grave-diggers, Maas Wally felt he understood something of Busha's desire for the solitude and isolation of Sylvan Hill as his final resting place.

The men paused to rest at the foot of Sylvan Hill. The peak had never seemed more far away. Then they began climbing, each man saving his strength so it could be spread out over the long climb. Fortunately it was still fairly cool, but they knew the heat of the sun would be on them before they were a third of the way up. At many points they had to use their machetes to cut their way through the thick vegetation. Spectacular views of the river, hills and mountains spread out below and around them as they climbed.

Breathing heavily, and covered with sweat, they finally got to the top. After a rest they began clearing the burial spot. Maas Wally, with his eye for measurements, began marking out the shape of the grave. Although it was unlikely that anyone was buried there, out of tradition they poured a bottle of white rum on the spot to appease the spirits.

Five of the men began digging. Uncle Charlie went into the bush in search of firewood and firestones. It was too soon to start cooking so he joined in the digging. But later in the morning he lit the fire, set the zinc-pan on the fire-stones and cooked yam, sweet potatoes, dumplings and salted pork. As the men dug, the excavated soil formed mounds around the grave.

At mid-day they ate their lunch in the shade of a tree at the edge of the hilltop.

Maas Wally cut off a bit of meat with his fork and said, "The setup will be Friday night and the funeral Saturday afternoon."

"We should all go to the setup too," said Maas Woody.

"I agree," said Bimrock.

After lunch Cutter smoked a cigarette and Uncle Charlie smoked his pipe; the other men stretched out on the grass.

Then, after drinking glasses of white rum, they resumed their digging. They all had other work commitments so they wanted to complete the grave in a day. The sun was nearing the top of the western hills when they got to the required depth of six feet. They put away their tools and began descending the hill, satisfied that the first half of their mission was completed.

All of them attended the setup at Busha's home the following Friday night. They sat with the rest of the large turnout in a booth made of bamboo and coconut fronds. There was an abundance of harddough bread, fried fish, coffee and rum. The six men joined in the singing. Uncle Charlie was an outstanding tenor, and Bimrock could hold his own as a bass in any setup anywhere.

Georgie Gee, finishing his third fish, turned to Maas Wally and said, "How did the digging go?"

"Fine."

"That was the easy part," said Georgie Gee. "Wait until you have to carry him up tomorrow."

"We will manage. We now have a feel of what the hill is like. We will have to pace ourselves."

The following afternoon, while the funeral service was in progress at the church, the six men – now pallbearers of the final leg – waited at the foot of Sylvan Hill. They wore their drudging clothes and hard boots. Cutter and Bimrock sat on a culvert.

Maas Wally, Uncle Charlie and Maas Woody sat on the grassy bank facing them. Scrutineer stood at the corner and whistled a funeral hymn while he watched the road on which the hearse would come; the men listened to him for he was a good whistler who knew many hymns.

The men heard later that the funeral was a grand affair with many dignitaries of the church, state and business sector attending. The church was packed and many people had to stand at the doors and in the churchyard. Members of the family sat in the traditional front row. Miss Ethel, dressed in black, was dry-eyed and stony-faced.

Frank was being seen in a suit, and in church, for the first time in many years. Cynthia had her hair covered with a black veil and sat beside her boyfriend and children. After the service some of Busha's relatives and close friends carried the coffin to the hearse.

When the six men heard the tolling of the bell they knew that the coffin was on its way. A small group of people had gathered at the bottom of the hill to watch the coffin begin the last leg of its journey. A few of them, because of curiosity, a sense of adventure or devotion to Busha, declared their intention to follow the coffin to the top of the hill.

The rector of the church was the first to arrive; he parked his car and got out. He was the first dark-skinned minister of the church and many described him as authoritarian and arrogant. His pouting lips and cold eyes indicated his displeasure at having to climb Sylvan Hill in order to perform the last rites over Busha Brandon.

The hearse arrived and the men received it and took up their positions: Maas Wally, Scrutineer and Bimrock on the left, and Uncle Charlie, Maas Woody and Cutter on the right. The rector led the way into the bushes and the men followed with some members of the small gathering behind them. "He won't be heavy," said Maas Wally, "he is going where he wants to go."

The men struggled and sweated. They made frequent stops to rest. There were times when some of them crawled on their stomachs to keep the coffin up; sometimes it slid backwards and they had to throw themselves on it to prevent it from sliding further. Two of the handles on the coffin broke off, making it more difficult to carry. Finally, soaked in sweat and covered with burr, they got to the top of the hill.

Bimrock went down into the grave to receive the coffin. The rector wiped the sweat from his face and went through the rites quickly. The men began covering the coffin with soil. The rector led the small gathering in the final hymn: *Pleasant are Thy Courts Above*. Dusk was fast approaching when they left Busha alone at his final retreat.

The following Monday morning, Maas Wally was on a ladder painting the outside of a house when he saw Cutter hurrying up the path towards the house.

"Maas Wally!" said Cutter, panting as he entered the yard. "I have something to tell you! Come down!"

"Gwaan and tell me, nuh."

"No man. Come down. You might drop off."

Maas Wally descended the ladder to the ground.

"The lawyer read Busha Brandon's will," said Cutter. "Busha said he would have no power over what his family decided to do with his body. But he wanted to be buried at the top of Sylvan Hill, and that if anyone decided to grant his wish, he was leaving a sum of money to be divided among the men who carried his body up there."

"What!" exclaimed Maas Wally. "Is plenty money?"

"A fair amount I hear."

"Bless my soul," said Maas Wally as he stepped off the ladder onto the ground.

That night The Waterbird Bar was full of men. The mood was festive. The six designated beneficiaries of Busha's will were buying drinks for everyone.

Georgie Gee kept shaking his head and muttering to himself. "Then the family don't object?" he asked.

"They weren't happy at first, but the lawyer told us they have decided to honour Busha's wishes," said Maas Wally. "And they going to stand the cost for us to build his tomb as well."

"I can buy a new suit for church and a dress for the wife," said Uncle Charlie.

"I need some new tools," said Maas Wally. "And I will be able to pay the children's school fees."

"I won't buy a new saw for sawyer work soon done," said Cutter. "But the money will help to set me up in a new trade."

"I going to bank that money," said Woody.

"I may get married to rahtid!" said Scrutineer, and everyone laughed.

Georgie Gee shook his head again. "Bumble-my-dee-and-bumble-my-dum!" he said.

She Knows His Body

After spending time as a farm-worker in the United States, Maas Boysie returns to the village and is asked the usual question:

"When you going back?"

"As soon as my bossman sends for me," he keeps replying. "He said he is going to send one letter to me, and another to the government so that nothing can hold me up."

So having confirmed the traveller's status the villagers expect from any sane man who has been overseas, he sets about acting the part. He wears only woollen shirts, blue jeans and leather boots with thick 'tractor' rubber soles. He is never seen anywhere without his leather cap with the turned-up ear flaps.

These flaps are useless in the warm Jamaican climate, but he thinks they look cool with the bow tied at the top of his head, and he pulls them down when the temperature drops below eighty and when it rains. When he wants to impress his listeners, he abandons his native creole language and speaks his own version of American. He spends hours sitting in the shops and on culverts discoursing on the superiority of life in America. As the days pass the streets of America get wider and wider; the speed of the traffic increases; the buildings get higher and higher; and the great, flat open spaces begin to stretch the credibility even of his willing audiences. "You have to go see for yourself how those white people wittify."

But Miss Dora, his wife, a calm church-going woman, does not like this role her husband is playing. She is sitting on a mortar in front of their small, bamboo kitchen, and she is shelling gungo peas into the chipped enamel bowl she has on her lap. She is thinking of the rough time her Boysie had getting that chance to go to America in the first place. The first time he went for the test he failed.

The examiner said he had too many bad teeth. So he sold one of his goats, went to a dentist and had his bad teeth taken out; then he put in a set of dentures which took the hollow out of his cheeks and made him look fresh and young again. The second time he went, the examiner told him to keep his knees stiff and touch his toes with his fingers, and when he could not do it, the examiner said "Sorry, pal, but you're not supple enough."

But instead of giving up, he started taking iron tablets and eating the few eggs faster than the fowls could lay them; and instead of drinking rum he turned to milk and stout and tonic wine. The third time the examiner squeezed his hands and said, "These hands too soft to do the white people's work."

Miss Dora is stirring the peas soup which is being cooked with yellow yam, dumplings and salt-pork. As she stirs the soup, the smoke rises past her face, escaping through the wattles and scraps of zinc that form the walls, or ascending to help form the stalactites of soot which hang from the roof. And she is thinking how lucky Boysie was to pass the test on his fourth try.

She remembers how happy he was when he came home from the test; he was so happy he kept saying over and over again that he was really going to America, as if he could not believe it. "You better pack my things because the call can come anytime now," he had said. She had washed his best clothes and had packed them. And true enough the telegram came just two days later and Boysie, dressed in the church clothes she had bought for him, but which he seldom wore, set off for America.

The soup is ready, and Miss Dora pours portions of it into bowls of varying sizes. As she fills each bowl she calls out the name of a child, going from the youngest to the oldest. On hearing his or her name each child appears, takes the bowl on the plate with the spoon, says 'Thanks mam', and goes into the house to eat, or sits in the shade of one of the trees. Miss Dora leaves Boysie's soup on the fire to keep it warm, and she is wishing he would come home early more often so they can eat together.

She is sitting on a stool on the verandah of the old wooden house which once belonged to Boysie's parents and she is eating while keeping an eye on the children. She is thinking that Boysie had brought back enough money for them to start building a house of their own beside the old one. She had put half of every dollar he had sent home in the bank which the government operated through the post office.

And she is thinking how nice it would be for Boysie to get another chance to make it easier, for things were getting rougher and rougher in the country. But she doesn't see how Boysie could get another chance. She knows his body better than anyone else and she knows that he isn't the man he used to be. His body is flabbier and he is beginning to show a paunch.

Even before he went to America, all those years of battering on the hillsides had started taking their toll on his body. And on top of that he had hurt his back lifting a sack in the States, and he had spent quite a bit of time in the hospital there.

But he keeps saying how the people were nice to him. "I was a hard worker," he keeps saying, "and they liked me for that. Sometimes the bossman would call me away from the work just to talk to me. He said he liked to hear me talk because I am a real jokify fellow." And thinking of how his body is, and the pain he still has in his back sometimes, she is wondering if much of their kindness wasn't just caution.

No, she isn't happy with this role Boysie is playing. While he talks about America, their few animals are 'reading newspapers' over the closely cropped grass, and his fields need the hands of a man. While he wanders around telling stories, the children – elevated with the novelty of wearing foreign clothes and being the children of a man who had travelled – now only want to eat food bought in the shop, and are becoming unruly show-offs.

A few months have passed and there is still no letter.

"It not going to come so soon, you know," Maas Boysie explains. "He is going to wait for the next crop to start. It take time for the crop to grow and be ready. And is reap they going to want me help them reap. They do most of their planting with machines. They not like us who still using our hands. And if the crop not so big he might not need as much help. That is how farming is: a big crop this year, a small one next year. But is only a matter of time. That letter could be in the mail tomorrow."

At Miss Dora's insistence, the building of the house begins. They make a digging and invite the men of the village. It is a moonlit night and the men sing digging songs while they prepare the level. When the level is ready they employ some carpenters to build the house.

The carpenters make building blocks with a mould. Then they begin mapping out the foundations. Maas Boysie wants a big house but Miss Dora persuades him to build a smaller one. They dig the foundations and begin raising the walls.

"It is a good thing we start," says Maas Boysie to his wife one night while they are in bed. "If the call comes before it finish, you can finish it yourself."

But there is still no sign of the airmail envelope. The postmistress says she is getting fed up with the Reynolds children. She says she is getting a cricked neck shaking her head at them. They've developed a kind of code so the children don't have to go all the way into the post office: as soon as she sees one of them approaching, she shakes her head or waves her hand, and the child turns and leaves.

She tells people she is hoping the infernal letter will arrive and give her some peace, and each evening she finds herself sorting the air mail envelopes first. But the months go by and the letter does not arrive. She tells the children to stop coming, that if the letter arrives she will send it along. The children tell their father what the postmistress said and it makes him angry. "What right has she to tell me when or when not to send for letters? Is her job to answer when she is asked. Is our tax-payers' money paying her. What a piece of facetiness! Pickney, oonu go ask for letter when I send oonu. And I hope she don't hold that letter when it come. She just the one to do it too. I know her. She don't come from anywhere, and those are the hardest people in the world." But the children avoid going to the post office, and lie when their father asks them.

The house is completed and they have an official opening. Maas Boysie delivers the main speech in his imitation American accent. He says that his first trip to the States was to build the house, the second would be to furnish it.

In the meantime other men in the village have got letters or tickets and have gone to the States. A few have returned. A little clique of ex-farmworkers is beginning to form in the village. They meet and compare their experiences. The younger men have newer and more exciting stories. They say that Maas Boysie had only scratched the surface. Gradually Maas Boysie is speaking less and less. The young men see him as a respected old-timer.

People notice he is beginning to wear some of his old clothes they had almost forgotten. The steep rocky hill-sides have destroyed his 'tractor' boots; the heavy basket he carries so regularly on his head has joined the sun and rain in destroying his cap with the ear flaps. Most of his jeans have been destroyed by the rough life of the bushes, and the few remaining ones are patched with pieces of his old clothes. One of the younger farm-workers has brought him a pair of blue jeans and a cap with the words 'Miami Dolphins' on it. He is very grateful and he wears them to the square on Saturday and Sunday evenings.

"It don't look as if that call coming, you know," he says to his wife one night. "I going to try to get a ticket."

His wife starts to say something but stops. She knows there is no use trying to dissuade him. So she just mentions that they prefer to give tickets to the younger men who have not yet had a chance.

"Young men?" exclaims Maas Boysie. "You mean these idle, good for nothing, young hooligans around the place? Six of them don't worth one of my hand. Any man who would choose one of them over me is a fool. This old horse not finished yet. I can work most of these young fellahs to a frazzle. I going to get a ticket. If the call come afterwards, that will be my bossman's bad luck. He can't say I didn't wait for him long enough. I am a patient and faithful man, but even a man like me have a limit."

A few months later he announces to his wife that he has got a ticket. "I had to oil his palm with a few dollars," he says, "but it going to pay off. I going to put some brand new furniture in this house for the enjoyment of you and the kids. I going to get a nice easy chair for you to rest your tired body in. I going to build a shed between the kitchen and house so you don't have to walk through the rain to bring food into the house. So help me, baby, I going to give you and the kids the life you really deserve."

The day before the test he asks his wife to pack his trunk. "Nowadays they don't give you much extra time like in the old days. As soon as you pass the test so bam, they putting you on the plane the same evening."

Later in the day he goes to the village barber and gets a haircut, sitting under a star apple tree beside the house. After dinner he has a bath. Then he goes to bed so early it makes his children nervous; they walk around the house whispering, afraid to shout or play.

The following morning he gets up early. His wife opens her eyes and sees him shadow-boxing before the mirror. He stops, then oils and brushes his hair.

"Mind the examiner think you are a sweet boy and send you back!" his wife says with a laugh from the bed.

"I going to face that examiner bright as morning sunshine," he says, doing a quick step. "And I going to talk to him about America so that he will know that I know that country. No point sending young fellas who don't know anything and have to learn from scratch. They should send men who know the place and the language. Men like me." And he flexes his biceps and throws back his head.

Miss Dora goes through the day quietly. She sends the children off to school and washes the clothes. Then she works in her vegetable garden and collects firewood. At mid-day she moves the goats and waters the cow. In the early afternoon she sews and rests a bit. By mid-afternoon she begins to prepare the evening meal.

She is thinking about Boysie and the test. She doesn't know what to think. She didn't expect him to get through the time he did and he had surprised her. Much as she doubts that he will get through, she finds it difficult not to hope that he will. But she wants to remain open to all possibilities, so she decides to prepare his favourite meal: mackerel and bananas and boiled St. Vincent yams.

The children return from school and ask about their father. She says she hasn't heard anything yet. They eat their dinner and go about their chores. Each time she hears the sound of a vehicle she prepares herself for the news. But he does not show up. She recalls that sometimes after the test, men return to the village in taxis at night with just enough time to get their trunks and rush back to Kingston to catch the plane. It is getting close to twilight. She puts his dinner on the table and waits.

It gets dark and she lights the lamp. A little boy, the child of a neighbour, comes to the house to borrow salt for his mother. As he turns to leave Miss Dora calls after him:

"You been out to the square, Byron?"

"Yes mam."

Miss Dora pauses. "You know if the men come back from the test yet?"

"Yes mam. They out at the shop."

She pauses again. "Maas Boysie out there?"

"Yes mam. He didn't pass, mam. Only two of them pass, mam. Robert and Quincey."

The boy runs off and she turns to go into the house.

"Papa don't pass!" she hears one of their daughters shouting to the others. "Papa fail! Papa fail!"

"Stop your shouting and do your homework!" she shouts at them.

The house is quiet as the children gather round the lamp with their books. Only Maas Boysie's dinner is still on the table. It is wrapped in a white towel, and a well-polished fork rests on top of it.

The night advances but he does not show up. She puts the children to bed. She sits up in bed and waits, and while she waits she reads a magazine she bought from a Jehovah's Witness travelling salesman. Maas Boysie does not come and she gets tired. She drifts off to sleep.

She wakes up when he enters the yard, and she can tell from his footsteps that he is drunk. She listens as he fumbles with the lock, opens the door and staggers inside. He pulls the chair from under the table, and the dishes rattle as he eats. Then there is a long silence. She feels herself drifting off to sleep again. When the silence continues she gets up and walks towards the dining room.

She stops at the door and peeps through the curtain. The plates are empty and he is no longer at the table. He is slumped in the old rocking chair, his head bowed, and from his dejected expression she can tell he is more drunk than asleep. She walks over, puts her hand at the back of his neck and shakes him gently. He lifts his head and stares, bleary-eyed.

"Come to your bed," she says as she holds him under his arms and tries to lift him.

He moans questioningly. She continues trying to lift him but he is very heavy. Finally, he manages to struggle to his feet, and he allows her to guide him along the wall towards the bedroom.

Miss Inez

Deaconess Carey did not have a car of her own with which to do her work. She could drive, and the church had offered her one, but she said she preferred to walk or use public transportation, as this was a way of keeping close to the people. She became a familiar figure on the streets and roads, slim and fair-skinned with freckles, and dressed in her blue and white uniform with her silver cross around her neck.

She and her husband lived in a cottage on the campus of the boarding school where she was based, and where she taught religious education and biology. But a good deal of her time was devoted to charitable work in the town and in the surrounding districts. It was also part of her job to coordinate religious activities in a number of other schools in the parish.

One morning she was on her way to the bus depot in the centre of the town. As she passed the market she saw a large crowd in the parking lot, and many of the people were laughing, cheering and shouting. She noticed that they were gathered around something that was happening in the centre, so she bored her way through the crowd to see what it was.

Two street people, a man and a woman, were struggling on the ground. The man had dreadlocks and dark-coloured clothes which were torn in many places, revealing his skin.

The woman was small and thin and her face was contorted; her head-tie was half-torn from her hair, and her ragged brown dress was pulled up to her thighs, revealing her naked legs. Her torn panty was lying on the ground beside her. The man had her pinned to the ground, and he was thrusting his buttocks as he tried to get his groin on top of hers.

Deaconess Carey realized with horror that the man was about to rape the woman, and that the crowd was cheering him on. She rushed over, grabbed the man by the waist and pulled him off the woman. The man stood up and glared at her, his eyes burning, the evidence of his lust bulging in his pants. For an instant she felt that he might attack her too, so she pressed both hands against his stomach and pushed him away.

"Go away! Get away!" shouted Deaconess Carey. "Look what you nearly did to this woman. And all you people stood by and did nothing. And some of you actually encouraged it. They may be mad, but they are people too, you know. What is happening to this society?"

The crowd began to disperse. Deaconess Carey heard someone in the crowd call her name, telling others who she was. The woman, who was now on her feet, ran over to the man and began pounding him with her fists. Deaconess Carey pulled her away from him.

"Come," she said. "Leave him alone. Do you know him?"

"No mam. I saw him on the street once or twice, but a short while ago was the first I ever said anything to him. And he attacked me right away."

The man began walking towards the street talking to himself about the weather. Most of the people were now gone. Only the vendors at the surrounding stalls continued to observe Deaconess Carey and the woman.

"Thank you, mam," said the woman, fixing her head-tie. She had a small face, gentle eyes, and a look of pride about her mouth. "I couldn't fight him off much longer. All the strength was going outa mi body."

"It would have been a horrible experience anywhere. But in a public place, surrounded by a cheering crowd!"

The woman began searching the ground for something. She picked up a small plastic container.

"Is mi medication," she said, putting the container into her pocket. "Me is all right when me take it. But sometimes it run out and me can't get none, or it lost. Me bring this from the hospital the other day and it soon finish too."

Deaconess Carey wondered what to do about the woman. Having just rescued her, she felt some responsibility for her, and did not feel right about simply returning her to the streets. She decided to postpone her visit to the school to which she was heading, and to spend some time seeing what she could do for the woman.

"Would you like a cup of tea or coffee?" she asked.

"Yes, mam. Me don't eat anything since morning, mam."

She led the woman back to her cottage.

Deaconess Carey served her fried eggs, toast and coffee, and joined her at the dining table with a cup of coffee for herself. The woman ate ravenously. After breakfast Deaconess Carey invited her to sit on the more comfortable sofa in the living room section. She pulled out the side tables and served two more cups of coffee for both of them.

"So tell me about yourself," said Deaconess Carey. "What is your name?"

"My name is Inez Wilson. Everybody used to call me Miss I. Now they call me only dirty names on the streets."

"I will call you Miss I."

"Is me one mi mother have. I didn't know mi father. And mi mother died when I was six. One of mi aunts raised me, and her children were like mi brothers and sisters. When mi age-up out of school I got a job as a maid with a bus owner in the district. I saved up and went to England.

"I worked hard in that cold country for twenty-odd years and I sent back money to one of mi cousins to save up for me. I asked her to buy a little piece of land and to build a house for me. She sent me a photograph of what she said was the house, and I returned to Jamaica only to discover that it was a fake photograph. It was a picture of somebody else's house. She used mi money to buy house and land for she and her man in their name. I was left with nothing but the few little possessions I brought back with me.

"I fret and fret and fret. I began to walk up and down the road. I couldn't sleep at night. Then I began to hear the voices in mi head. I heard the voices of people I knew and people I didn't know. They cursed me and traced me and told me I was worthless. They command me to do things. Some were the most evil things I have ever heard and they threatened to kill me.

"The voices went on non-stop day and night. The whole world was crackling with them. I would lie in bed day and night listening to them. I cut myself off from the rest of the world. When they dragged me out and I told them what the voices were saying they laughed at me. Next thing they took me to a doctor who sent me to the mental hospital. When I came out my relatives rejected me. I ended up on the streets. From time to time one of them will come and catch me and carry me back to the hospital. But when they discharge me I am soon back on the streets again. For none of them want me."

"How irresponsible!" said Deaconess Carey.

Miss Inez looked up at a framed picture on the wall. "Is that you and your husband and daughter?"

"Yes. My husband works with a bauxite company and comes home on weekends. My daughter is at university."

"I had a son when I was in England. But he died. He is now buried under the snow."

She began crying softly.

"Cry it out, Miss I," said Deaconess Carey, "cry it out."

Miss Inez put her face in her hands and wept some more.

"I am going to try and help you," said Deaconess Carey. "In the meantime you can stay here. I am going to fix up the helper's quarters for you. It has its own bathroom. I suggest you have a bath right now, as a matter of fact. You are about my daughter's size so some of her dresses should fit you. Come let's fix up the place. You can wash and clean, can't you?"

"Yes, mam. Me used to work as a chamber maid in a hotel in England."

The following day Deaconess Carey took her to a doctor in Kingston; they travelled on the school bus which was making one of its trips to the city. The doctor examined her and prescribed medication; he also gave her a letter to be taken to a psychiatric nurse who worked at the public hospital in the town in which Deaconess Carey lived. Deaconess Carey took her to see the nurse the following day. The nurse had a programme of occupational therapy for the mentally ill, and Deaconess Carey enrolled Miss Inez in it; Miss Inez opted to learn sewing, a skill she could practise on her own.

A white Volkswagen rolled into the Carey's carport the following Friday evening and Mr. Carey came out. He was big, brown-skinned and had straight hair, and he looked scholarly in his horn-rimmed glasses. He took a suitcase from the back-seat and knocked on the door. Deaconess Carey opened the door and he kissed her on the lips and passed her on his way to their bedroom. In the passage he met Miss Inez who was carrying a broom.

"Good evening," he said. "And who are you?"

"This is Miss I," said his wife behind him. "I will tell you about her later."

"Is she a helper?"

"In a way, yes."

It was while they were in bed that night that Deaconess Carey told her husband about Miss Inez.

"You brought a mad woman into the house?" exclaimed Mr. Carey, springing up in bed.

"Listen! Listen! Hear me out."

"But she could be dangerous! She could burn down the house! She could murder us both!"

"The doctor said she isn't dangerous. He said people with her illness are among the gentlest people in the world. She is safer than many of the so-called sane people around you everyday."

"And she could have all kinds of diseases. You picked her up off the streets!"

"The doctor examined her. He said he found no evidence of anything physically wrong with her."

"He could be wrong. We will have to take her back to Bellevue. It is the government's business to take care of people like that."

"They don't have the space there. They can accommodate only the new ones coming in. As soon as they are well enough they discharge them."

"Well, what about her relatives?"

"They rejected her."

"And we must do what they refuse to do?"

"The people from the byways and hedges, my dear. Ours is a radical and difficult faith. Remember my vows."

"But surely she isn't going to be here forever."

"I plan to go into her district one day to see if I can find a relative who will have her. But first we have to find a way by which she can support herself and get regular medical attention. I want to see her live like a free and responsible person."

Mr. Carey said nothing more, but she could tell from the way he tossed and turned that he slept uneasily that night.

Deaconess Carey discussed Miss Inez's situation with the principal of the school, the nurse and guidance counsellor. The principal suggested a concert to raise funds for Miss Inez. They put the idea to the students who responded warmly. The students went further: they decided to miss one meal on an agreed on day so that the money saved could go into the fund. The concert was a success. When Miss Inez, who had a lovely voice, sang "Pass me not, o gentle saviour", tears sprang in Deaconess Carey's eyes.

Some months later, on a Saturday afternoon, Deaconess Carey and her husband set off in the Volkswagen for Dripping Spring, Miss Inez's home district. They left her at home for they did not want to discuss their plans with her yet, and they felt that her presence might prejudice their enquiries.

When they got to the village they stopped and requested information from some of the persons they saw walking on the road, but most of the responses were not very helpful. A Rastafarian who was wearing a red tam and driving a goat in front of him suggested that they enquire at the shop which was further up the road on their left. When they got to the shop they decided to speak to the shopkeeper.

As they went inside they greeted a chubby woman in a knitted blouse who was sitting on a bench on the piazza. Then they greeted the shopkeeper who was a smiling, round-faced woman with gold teeth. They began asking for the whereabouts of some of the persons whose names they had picked up from Miss Inez's conversations. The shopkeeper was guarded at first, but Deaconess Carey noticed that her manner softened somewhat after she glanced at the cross she was wearing.

"Is Inez Wilson's family you looking for, mam?" asked the woman who was sitting on the piazza.

"Yes," said Deaconess Carey.

"Is long time we don't hear anything about her."

"She is living with us."

"With you, mam?"

"Yes. She is doing well with her dressmaking, and getting good orders from a friend of ours who owns a boutique. But we don't think she should be cut off from her relatives."

"She used to be very sick, mam."

"Yes, but she is a lot better now. She can help herself, and she has something to offer."

The shopkeeper said, "Oldtime people say what don't dead, don't throw away."

"That is so true," said Deaconess Carey.

"Me is her second cousin, mam," said the woman on the piazza.

The second cousin's name was Mrs. Fay Henry, and she said everybody called her Aunty Fay. Deaconess

Carey invited her to visit Miss Inez. A warm relationship gradually developed between the two women. Miss Inez, anxious to show off her new skills and her new friends, and homesick for the familiar people and places of her childhood, agreed to return to the village to live with Aunty Fay.

Several months went by. One Saturday evening, as was her custom, Deaconess Carey was in her kitchen cooking beef soup and roasting beef for their Sunday dinner. Mr. Carey was in the study sorting out bills. There was a knock on the door and Deaconess Carey went to see who it was. She saw a smiling Miss Inez in a red and white floral dress, and a gentle-eyed man in a felt hat, blue shirt and grey trousers. Miss Inez was carrying a brown-paper parcel under her arm.

"Good evening, Deaconess," said Miss Inez. "This is my friend Mr. Tomlinson."

"Friend? You mean boyfriend?"

Miss Inez giggled and the man smiled.

"Yes, mam. Me not dead yet, you know. Besides dem say that the older the coconut tree the sweeter the juice."

They all laughed.

"Come inside," said Deaconess Carey. "Would you like a cup of tea?" she asked when they were seated.

"Thank you, mam," said Miss Inez.

Deaconess Carey went into the kitchen and put on the kettle. While she was waiting for it to boil she sat on the easy chair facing Miss Inez and Mr. Tomlinson.

"So Mr. Tomlinson, what do you do for a living?" she asked.

"Farming. I have a piece of land and a house. Mi wife died three years ago. If you use your head you can find your way in farming. Me love the farming bad. But the younger generation don't want it. The other day I told one of them who was idling to go and farm. He told me that the only way his hand touch the ground, him must fall down."

Mr. Tomlinson's gold teeth gleamed as he laughed at his joke, and Miss Inez and Deaconess Carey joined him in his mirth.

Mr. Carey came into the living room.

"Nice to see you, Miss I," he said shaking her out-stretched hand. Miss Inez introduced Mr. Tomlinson and they shook hands.

"Join us for tea," Deaconess Carey said to her husband. When the tea was ready she served it with slices of corn-meal pudding.

"I have a present for both of you," said Miss Inez after tea was finished. She handed the parcel to Deaconess Carey.

"Oh, you shouldn't be giving us presents, Miss I," said Deaconess Carey as she opened the package. It contained a white blouse and a blue shirt. "They are lovely!"

"My own design," said Miss Inez.

"They are very nice," said Mr. Carey, "but you really ought to be saving your money you know."

"Good friend better than pocket money," said Miss Inez.

"They will mean a lot to us," said Deaconess Carey.

As they were leaving, Deaconess Carey noticed, with approval, that Mr. Tomlinson opened the door for Miss Inez.

After supper that evening Deaconess Carey offered her husband a glass of her homemade pimento liqueur. She was proud of her liqueur, and her husband and visitors often said it was the best they had ever tasted. They relaxed in their seats facing each other and enjoyed their drink.

"I wonder what happened to that would-be rapist?" said Deaconess Carey.

Mr. Carey choked on his liqueur. "I hope you are not thinking of bringing him here as well."

"I hadn't thought of it. But now that you mentioned it..."

When she saw the look on her husband's face she burst out laughing; she laughed harder than she had for a very long time.

"He could use some of the medication, though," she said, "and some of the occupational therapy."

"No sewing or basket making for him. He should be given a sledge hammer to break rockstone."

"I have been reading up on mental illness. I think I am going to devote more of my time to it. Did you know that so far there is no general agreement on what it is exactly? Is it an inherited defect in brain chemistry and therefore really a bodily disease? Or is it a defect in the personality caused by faulty upbringing? Or is it simply socially deviant behaviour?"

"They used to think it was possession by demons, didn't they?"

"Yes, but we've come a long way from demons."

Silence fell on the house as Deaconess Carey and her husband meditated over their liqueur. They were thinking about the empty helper's quarters. And of Miss Inez and Mr. Tomlinson somewhere out in the night, resisting the fears of centuries.

Hurricane Story

"**H**oy Mr. Evans!" came a woman's voice from the road, "you don't hear that a hurricane coming?" Patrick looked up from the bicycle chain he was oiling and saw Mrs. Mary Grossett standing at the entrance to the yard, her opulent frame almost filling the opening in the hibiscus hedge. She had a round, kind face and she was dressed for church in a white dress and white hat, and she had a handbag strapped under her left arm.

"Hurricane?" said Patrick, "which hurricane?"

"You stay there. A big, bad hurricane heading straight for Jamaica. It supposed to hit the island tomorrow morning. You don't listen to your radio?"

"Cho! Nearly all my life I been hearing that hurricane coming. And they always swing north before they get here."

"We going to pray at church for this one to swing away as well. And it might swing away too, yes. In spite of what they saying, God can do anything. But if it to come it going to come. So prepare yourself. They say all churches and schools will be used as shelters."

Patrick stood up and looked into the sky. There was indeed a wild and ominous look to the clouds. Earlier, the overcast sky had made him wonder if he would be able to visit his parents the following day, the first day of his vacation. His parents lived in the eastern hills, four parishes away.

"Watch and pray, Mr. Evans," said Mrs. Gossett as she began climbing the hill.

Patrick put the bicycle in the shed which his landlord, a cabinet maker, used as his workshop. Then he went into his room. He was alone in the house, for his landlord and his wife were in the United States visiting their children. Their part of the house was locked away and he would be unable to get inside there in the event of a hurricane.

There was religious music on the radio, but he let it play to see if there would be any bulletins. He sat on the more comfortable of his two chairs and looked around the room wondering what he should pack should it become necessary for him to leave. It was a cosy room and, according to his landlady, well kept for a man's room.

There was a single bed covered with a bedspread with a floral design at the centre and at the corners; a bedside mat made from straw with an oriental design; a table with his lamp, kerosene stove and utensils; a hanging press with his clothes and under which was his suitcase; and a bookshelf filled with books. At the end of the service a bulletin confirmed what Mrs. Gossett had said. There was also advice on the precautions to be taken.

Patrick went to a nearby shop and bought bread, crackers, sardines, nuts, fruits, candles, matches, flashlight batteries and kerosene oil. His landlord's tools were locked away so he was unable to batten down any of the windows. He began packing his suitcase; he put in clothes, toiletries, food, valuable documents which he wrapped in plastic, and two books on religion.

That night he lay in bed listening to the wind howling. The house felt lonelier than it had ever been, with his landlord's and landlady's belongings in their silent rooms, far away from the persons who gave them significance, and who were probably unaware of the impending hurricane, and even if they knew, were impotent to do anything about them now. He listened to the wind increasing in intensity as the night advanced.

There had been a hurricane one night when he was a boy, but he had slept through it. He remembered waking up to an abundance of water coconuts, sugar cane and corn, and with so much food around he had thought then that a hurricane wasn't such a bad thing. While growing up he had yearned to experience one, and often felt disappointed when they turned from the island.

His mother used to chide him for longing for hurricanes: "Young bird don't know hurricane until him grow up and it blow him away," she used to say. An avid reader, he had read about them at school, and in books borrowed from the library where he worked as an assistant, and he knew now that they were dangerous.

The following morning after breakfast he sat with his door open and watched the approaching storm. The dishevelled trees were like distraught mourners bending in distress. He noticed a ripe passion fruit swinging on a vine which had almost covered a tree on the other side of the road. He waited to see the fruit fall, but it held on tenaciously. Watching the tossing fruit, he remembered the peace and calm of the previous Saturday. He had gone to the beach with friends, and he could remember what it was like floating on his back in the calm sea and looking up at the peaceful blue sky.

Nothing had been further from his mind then than the possibility that two days later he would be facing a hurricane. He shifted his attention from the fruit for a few minutes. When his eyes searched for it again it was gone. The wind had torn off the branch which was now lying on the ground. The hurricane had struck its first blow in his vicinity.

He locked the door and turned his attention to the radio. The announcer said that the hurricane was now battering the eastern end of the island, and it was expected to move westwards across the country. In the interest of safety, the electricity company had cut off its supply of power. Seventeen persons were already reported dead.

People were calling the station with appeals for help. An old people's home had lost its roof and the matron was asking people in the neighbourhood to offer refuge to its now homeless residents. Several children had been washed away in a gully which ran through an inner-city area. A woman who was in labour, and whose street was blocked by a fallen utility pole, was appealing for the help of a doctor. Gangs of armed looters were raiding business places and the homes of persons who had fled to shelters.

He took a book by David Hume from his shelf and using his flashlight, found the quote that had been running through his mind:

"Is he [God] willing to prevent evil, but not able? Then he is impotent. Is he able, but not willing? Then he is malevolent. Is he both able and willing? Whence then is evil?"

Patrick thought about the ruined nursing home. Why would God do that to sick, old people? He pondered over this question but could find no answer.

The callers on the radio were now joking about the hurricane. One said they should name it 'Rufus' because of all the roofs it was blowing off. The station began playing songs like, 'Don't Worry Be Happy', 'Enjoy Yourself' and 'Happy Days Are Here Again'.

Patrick listened to the rain pelting the zinc roof with varying degrees of intensity. It was easy to imagine an angry, primitive will behind it all. One of the books in the library said that naming them was a coping mechanism, in that humanizing them made it easier to deal with them. It was the same impulse, the book said, behind the gods of the world's mythologies. One of the callers said he saw the hurricane as punishment for the country's alarming murder rate.

Another said she saw God in the hurricane, as only the existence of such a being could explain such violent destructiveness. But to Patrick there was no need to imagine anything beyond the storm; for him it was enough that the universe was capable of behaving in those ways. His mind was focused on the water on the roof and the wind under the eaves.

Later, the radio reports indicated that the hurricane was now passing over his area. He knew the names of the prominent people whose houses had reportedly lost their roofs. The mayor of the town came on the air and appealed for calm; he also asked for volunteers to help at the hospital which was badly damaged and flooded. The wind seemed to be whistling around the house. It was followed by what sounded like a huge tidal wave crashing over the roof.

There were sounds he had never heard or imagined: fighting dinosaurs, a train gone mad, a siren on the Hell Express. Then he heard a succession of loud rips as the wind tore the zinc from the roof of his house. The ceiling of masonite quickly followed as the rain poured heavily into his room. Within a few seconds he was soaked to the skin, and he could feel the water rising on the floor and getting into his shoes.

He was surprised at how calm he was; it was like watching himself in a movie. He shoved a few things under the table, slipped a few more items into his suitcase and went outside. With his suitcase on his head, he walked against the wind which was so strong he felt it would lift him from the earth at any moment. With the wind now behind him, he began climbing the hill toward the church.

Muddy water rolled heavily down the path adding to the sponginess of his shoes. The shop now looked as if it had been splashed by the foot of a marauding giant; it was now a mangled pile of wood, zinc, mesh wire and bush. Half-way up the hill he looked down to where the land sloped to the plain. Sheets of zinc were flying in the air with enough force to decapitate anyone in their path. Where the edge of the town extended to the plain, he could see dozens of roofless houses with fallen trees and scattered bits of roofing material lying between them. Most trees were without leaves, and the land around him was covered with a disorder of twisted and broken trunks and branches. He could now see houses he had never seen before, smashed houses exposed to the public for the first time.

Patrick arrived at the church at the top of the hill. He went through the two iron pillars which were the remnants of a gate and approached the covered entrance of the church. He could hear the seekers of shelter in the church singing the hymn 'A Mighty Fortress Is Our God'. He found the Rev. G. Ephraim Guthrie and a few other male officials standing in the entrance. The Rev. Mr. Guthrie was a tall, brown man with European features and was considered handsome by his female parishioners. He was wearing his collar, a windbreaker and water-boots. He gave Patrick a searching stare.

"I come for refuge," said Patrick, removing the suitcase from his head and putting it on the floor. "The wind blew off mi roof."

"Do you know him?" asked the Rev. Mr. Guthrie, turning to the other men.

"Him live with the Rainfords," said one of the men.

"Are you a member of this church?" asked the minister.

"No," said Patrick.

"I didn't think so. Are you the member of any church?"

"No."

"Well, this is a refuge for church members only. We can't fill up the place with non-members and leave no space for members who might need it."

"But this is a hurricane!" protested Patrick.

"You should have thought of that when you decided not to join a church," said the minister. He turned to the men. "They come to be christened, married and buried. But between those times you don't see them at all. Unless there is a hurricane." He turned back to Patrick. "There is no place here for you, sir!"

Patrick put the suitcase back on his head and walked out into the swirling rain. He decided to try the school. "Is my taxes keep up that," he said to himself. "They can't turn me away from there."

At the church gate he heard what sounded like several gunshots followed by a long, creaking sound. Then there was an enormous moan of terror which rose above the howling and crackling of the hurricane. He turned and saw most of the roof of the church rolling and falling to pieces down the hillside.

It was followed by a huge chunk of cut-stone wall. The covering of the entrance was also gone, and Patrick saw the Rev. G. Ephraim Guthrie running awkwardly with his long legs toward his residence which, fortunately for him, was on the other side of the hill. Cries of panic and confusion were coming from the church, and people were pouring out of the hole in the cut-stone wall, the windows and doors, many with their belongings on their heads and under their arms.

Patrick continued on his way. Why would God destroy a church? he wondered. The wind had dismantled the roof to which his praises had risen for years; wind and rain were now washing debris down to the places where the faithful had prayed. The walls, built by devout hands long ago, were crumbling.

The universe is indifferent to theology, he said to himself as he felt the rain stinging his face. It didn't care anything about the minister's lack of charity or the faith of those who were singing and praying. What is a priest before a hurricane? he asked himself rhetorically. And he chuckled at the memory of the Rev. G. Ephraim Guthrie, now soaked like the rest of them, rushing home to save his own skin first.

On his way down the hill he met Mrs. Grossett and her husband and three children carrying suitcases and baskets.

"What a hurricane eh Mr. Evans!" said Mrs. Grossett. "Absolutely the worst one I have ever seen. Took off our roof like paper. Seen what it did to yours too. We heading for the church."

Patrick told them about the church.

"Have mercy! Have mercy!" cried Mrs. Grossett. "How is Miss Pinnock's house?"

"Roof still on," said Patrick.

Miss Pinnock was a postmistress and a friend of the Grossetts.

"I know they will take us in," said Mrs. Grossett. "All things work for good for them that love the Lord, Mr. Evans. For everything give thanks. He is sending us this to build our souls."

Build souls indeed, thought Patrick, thinking of the armed, marauding looters and the minister.

"Hope Miss Pinnock's roof is still on," he said as he continued down the hill.

He stood in the rain in front of his home and looked at the roofless building and the debris in the yard. In that home he had eaten and slept; enjoyed the company of his former girlfriend who had left him after he had refused to join her church; and where he had read the many books he had borrowed and bought.

Now water was pounding the place of all those memories, and the world which had been his, only a few days before, now seemed very far away. The shed was flattened, but now was not the time to try and salvage his bicycle; it was probably safer from looters under there. The Rainfords had left a telephone number, and if the lines were open he would call them after the hurricane. Patrick walked along potholed roads, streets and avenues strewn with fallen power lines, rocks, bottles, old tyres and other debris.

At the school, he was assigned to one of the classrooms in the men's section. Several men and boys were already there. Patrick pushed four desks against a wall to make a bed, changed into dry clothes and stretched out to rest.

He noticed a tall, young man in a white cap removing books from a case and using them to form a mattress on the floor. "You want some?" he asked Patrick. Patrick thought about it for a few moments. He had a reverence for books and felt that using them in this way was beyond him. "No thanks," he said. The young man stretched out on the books and within seconds was snoring aloud.

"When I was coming here a tree fell across the road and missed me by so," said an old man in pants and a vest.

"Thirty-seven dead already," said a man in a red cap. "But it could be worse still. We haffi give thanks."

What about the dead and injured? Patrick wondered as he turned on his back and looked up at the roof. Are they to give thanks too?

Patrick turned on his radio. The hurricane was now battering the western end of the island. The resort areas there had already suffered a lot of damage. All overseas lines were down, and except for ham radio operators, the island was now isolated from the rest of the world.

In the evening persons in the shelter were served bread, sardines, corned beef and lemonade. It rained heavily throughout the longest and darkest night Patrick had ever known. In the morning the radio reports said that the hurricane, still gathering momentum, was now on its way to the Mexican coast.

After breakfast the Rev. G. Ephraim Guthrie arrived to conduct a service for them in the schoolyard. Patrick did not go. From the volume of the singing he could tell that the service was well attended. And he could hear the minister's strong voice reading his text: "I was a stranger, and ye took me in." Matthew 25:35-36.

After the service, word went around the shelter that, according to a radio report, members of parliament would be distributing zinc to the roofless. Patrick decided that on his way to his home to salvage what he could from his room, he would take the long route so he could stop at the MP's office and put his landlord's name on the list of persons needing zinc. There was a big crowd there but after a long wait he was able to get the name and address on the list. Then he set off for home via the road that passed the church.

As he passed it he was surprised to hear organ music coming from the damaged place of worship. He went to the door and looked inside. High on the altar, above all the rubble, Mrs. Grossett was playing the organ. A surviving bit of roof had protected it from the rain. Mrs. Grossett was singing fervently as she played the Tate and Brady hymn:

Through all the changing scenes of life
In trouble and in joy
The praises of my God shall still
My heart and tongue employ.

Patrick observed the scene with astonishment. Then he left quietly, not wanting to disturb her. The religious impulse, he said to himself, is a strong and amazing thing.

In front of his house he noticed that the branch with the passion fruit was still on the ground. He picked it up. The passion fruit was sour, but it made one of the most delicious drinks he knew. He thought of the seeds inside. Let them grow, he said to himself, thinking of the lush, green island he once knew, and for which he now felt a great nostalgia. There was life and death on the earth and the two were inextricably linked. That was all he knew, and it was probably the basis for all the world's religions. And with a yearning for the green life to come again, he threw the fruit into the cultivation.

His Mother's Religion

aniel saw the light in his mother's room, and he knew that she was getting ready to go to the Christmas-morning service. He did not want to go with her. His experiences of life, combined with his wider reading, had damaged his earlier religious faith, and he now found most church services dull and depressing. But he had returned to the village proudly driving a car of his own, and he did not see how he could lie in bed and let his mother walk a mile or so to church.

For a few minutes he lay in bed and watched the light in his mother's room. He knew that light well. During his childhood it was the light of his mother's prayers and devotional readings, and it indicated that she was getting ready for her day's labours. Those labours included preparing his breakfast so he could get to school on time, and he knew that her efforts had eventually made virtually every good thing in his life possible. Watching the light now, he sensed the significance of religion in his mother's life, and he wanted to at least help her do that which was so important to her. He got out of bed and started getting ready.

Neither mother nor son said a word as they shared their breakfast of a halved navel-orange and hot cups of sweet mint tea. Daniel studied his mother's dark, strong face in the light of the kerosene lamp, but he saw no indication that she was responding to his unsolicited and unexpected decision. They disagreed on most religious matters, but they no longer argued about them. Religion lay dormant in the unspoken area of their relationship.

A short while later they began walking up the hillside path towards the main road. There was no driveway to their house, which had been built with no thought of future modern conveniences like cars, and his car was parked on a side road near the home of some of their relatives. Daniel walked behind his mother and guided her footsteps with his flashlight. The air was pleasantly chilly, and he was quickly losing all nostalgia for the warm bed he had left behind.

They paused for rest, and as he looked up at the stars he gasped at the sight of their immeasurable abundance, and their apparent closeness to the earth. Living in the city he had forgotten about starry country nights. Christmas, he thought, was also about stars. One Christmas morning, when he was a child, his mother's helper told him that the morning star he was seeing was the star of Bethlehem, and he could still remember the sense of awe and mystery that the thought had evoked in him.

His reading in astronomy had demystified some of his feelings about stars, and he now knew of the doubts about the astronomical claims made about Christmas. At times the cosmos that he studied seemed like a vast and godless place. At other times the micro-world seemed more like mind than matter. But now as he climbed the hillside, and seemed to be moving closer and closer to the stars, he felt some of his childhood feelings coming back to him. His studies had not destroyed his sense of the awe and mystery of it all.

While he wiped the dew from the windscreen, he could hear his mother knocking on the door of the house which was a short distance below the road. She was having some difficulty waking their relatives. Daniel reflected on how things had changed. When his grandparents lived in that house, their relatives used to travel from all over the island to be with them on Christmas Eve.

They decorated the house with bunches of oranges and tangerines, filled the coppers with water, and stocked the house with food and drink. They feasted all night and sang carols to the accompaniment of the banjo that one of his uncles played. Then when it was morning they went to the service at the church. Now he heard his mother knocking at the door of a house that, in its Christmas-morning silence, seemed to belong to another age.

Daniel sat in his car and turned on the radio. Carols flowed in an unbroken stream from a flashier and more glittering world, and they described a Christmas that seemed out of his reach. He once regarded the extraordinary beauty of Christmas music as evidence for the season's supernatural origins.

Now he was of the view that the people of Christendom had given Christmas their best tunes, and they did so because they liked what it said to them. Still, he enjoyed the idea of his new car transmitting this ancient music on a dark and lonely side road in a rural village. He enjoyed the novelty of the situation so much that he reached over and turned up the volume.

His mother returned, triumphantly escorting some of their relatives. She got in beside him, and by the roof-light he had a quick glimpse of the others as they slipped into the back seat and closed the doors. There were three of them: Aunt Ruth who was always cheerful;

Mark, a cousin he barely recognized because of his new afro; and a dark youth of about his own age whom his aunt introduced as Philip, the husband of one of his distant cousins.

"Glad to see you, Dan-Dan," said his aunt as she squeezed his shoulder affectionately.

"And we get to taste the new car," said Mark.

The drive to the church was, for Daniel, a journey along the most memory-filled bit of roadway in his life. He had travelled on that road from his time in his mother's womb, he felt sure, until the time he graduated from high school. It was the road to education on week-days, and the road to religion on weekends. Nearly every bit of that road, every curve, culvert and tree, evoked some remembered incident.

Now, as they drove along the winding road in a car alive with carols and talk of Christmas, it seemed as if the car's headlights were deliberately picking out the images of Christmas. He saw groves of ripening oranges on the hillsides, sugar-cane flags with their indigenous shapes of Christmas trees, and fields of sorrel that produced the season's wine.

Daniel approached the church with stars, carols, and the Christmas lore of the village on his mind.

But they found the churchyard empty, and the church was locked and in darkness.

"Who is supposed to conduct this service?" Mark demanded as he left the car.

"Parson said he would be here at five o'clock," Daniel's mother assured them.

"So more people should be here by now," said Mark as he read the luminous dial of his watch. "It is nearly time."

The others got out of the car and, following Daniel's mother, they walked over to the brow of the hill over-looking the main road and the neighbouring villages. From there they could see the dark surrounding hills which were silhouetted against the starry skies. But there were no lights in the villages from which they expected people to come.

The minister of the church, Daniel recalled, lived some twenty hill-and-gully miles away in the dark hills, and he had several churches closer to where he lived. He would travel the distance to join them, Daniel felt, only if that dark and deserted church occupied some special place in his spiritual affection. For several minutes, the small group stood silently together and brooded over the dark villages in front of them.

"Boy, this place mash up bad," said Mark. "I remember what this place used to be like when I was small. The churchyard would be packed by now. And from up here you could see people marching to the service with candles. You could see them coming from all around, and you could hear them singing carols, and they would all meet and line up below here at the gate, and when the minister arrive he would lead the procession up the hill into the church. Now look how the place dead!"

There is a special kind of sadness, thought Daniel, in the nostalgia of the young.

"Merry Christmas everybody!"

The booming voice of a man came out of the darkness on their right, and a dark figure came closer to them.

The voice was familiar to Daniel, and although he was not absolutely sure, he linked it with a prominent figure in one of the local pocomania churches.

"Where is the caretaker?" the stranger demanded, speaking with some authority. "By now the church should be open and blazing with light. The man is not doing his job! And you know why he is not doing his job? Because nobody wants his job. In this country, beware of a man with a safe job."

The stranger had a flair for monologue, and he launched a satirical attack on the absent caretaker. His voice was strong and domineering, and he tolerated no interruptions. The rest of the group stood in silence and listened to his economic, psychological and religious critique of the caretaker's shortcomings.

Later they heard the caretaker's keys rattling to the rhythm of his long strides. Then they heard his footsteps mounting the steps to the vestry. They followed him up the dark steps.

"Why oonu didn't ring the bell?" he turned and shouted angrily at them. He fumbled with the lock and berated them under his breath. "Not one of them with enough sense to ring the bell. Studderation better than education anytime, I tell you. Studderation make you ring the bell; education make you wait."

Mark left to ring the bell.

The caretaker finally managed to open the door, and they followed him into the dark vestry. He had an unlighted gas lamp with him, and with the help of Daniel's flashlight, he searched a drawer for the materials he needed to light it. He could not find them, and when the search seemed hopeless, he hissed his teeth and closed the drawer.

"It look like me leave dem a yard," he said.

"Not enough studderation," said the stranger.

The caretaker ignored his comment and marched out of the vestry, carrying the lamp with him.

Daniel's mother led them into the nave of the church, and they felt their way to the front benches. They sat in the dark and listened to Mark ringing the bell. The caretaker, Daniel recalled, lived about a half-a-mile away. They could only hope that he knew where to find his materials.

"People say I do all kinds of terrible things," said the stranger as he attempted another monologue. "I was born and raised in that church, and now everybody turning against me. But I can always find a church."

The stranger could not keep his voice above the sound of the bell, and most of what he said was lost on Daniel. But the ringing of the bell did not prevent him from speaking. Being inside the church, it seemed, induced a confessional mood, and he talked about segments of his life, hinting at the dark accusations which he said were being levelled against him by the members of his former church.

Gradually, a few newcomers joined them. Daniel recognized two of them by their voices. One was the shopkeeper who lived near the church-gate; she was a member of another church which was about a mile away, and she was probably choosing the nearer church because of its convenience. The other was a returned immigrant from England who, after many years back in the village, still remained a remote and distant figure. Daniel did not recognize the woman with the two children, or the woman who came alone and sat by herself behind them.

It was, for Daniel, a strange feeling sitting in a dark church waiting to see if a service would happen. He thought of the organ music in the carols on the radio, and he imagined big cathedrals full of people, music and light. When his thoughts returned to the dark and lonely space around them, Christmas never seemed further away.

The ringing of the bell stopped and they heard voices outside. Then a light appeared in the vestry, and a man walked towards them with a lighted gas lamp swinging by his knees. Mark followed him and together they pulled a table from against the wall and placed it in front of the small gathering. The man placed his lamp on the table, and Mark joined the congregation.

"Good morning, friends," said the lamp-bearer in what sounded like an American accent. "It is already late and Minister not here yet. I woke up with a feeling that he might be late or not show up at all, so I came prepared to at least start the service. I also had a feeling there might be no lamp," he glanced towards the vestry and chuckled, "so I brought a little light of my own."

Daniel recognized the stand-in preacher as Andre, a former theology student who was trained by American missionaries. After giving up his training for the ministry, he worked in Cuba for a number of years, and he still retained the habit of wearing Cuban-style bush-jackets.

"My friends," the preacher continued, "I know that I am not worthy to conduct this service. I am, as they say, living in sin with my woman. But it is because we are sinners why we are here."

"Amen brother!" said the stranger.

"Don't be discouraged by our small number," said the preacher. "The first Christmas was not an over-crowded event either."

He led them through a round of badly sung carols. They sang without musical accompaniment, and they were unfamiliar with each other's voices. Daniel shone his flashlight in his mother's hymn book so she could see. But he did not join in the singing. He found it hard to sing words he did not believe in. There was not enough light from the preacher's lamp for all of them to see, so the preacher read each line of the hymns aloud before they sang it. They were used to this kind of singing from nine-nights and wakes, so they soon fell into a comfortable rhythm.

While one of the lessons was being read, Daniel looked around at the interior of the church. The walls and columns seemed freshly painted; a concrete floor had replaced the wooden one of former years; and there was a new pulpit on a pedestal of concrete. The building was in better shape than he remembered it as a child, but it seemed as if material well-being had out-distanced attendance.

Daniel began thinking about the church, a magnificent building in a remote inland village, built at a time, he felt sure, when it was surrounded mostly by shacks. It was still by far the most splendid building for miles around. Few, if any, of the present villagers knew anything about its history, although he had heard his mother say that her grandmother used to speak of carrying stones on her head as a child to help build it.

The colonizing powers had erected it to promote a point of view relayed through empires from ancient Palestine to this far away district. Now the church, with so many untold stories in its silent, enduring walls, was witnessing this tiny Christmas service, a mere flicker of the flame it was erected to nurture.

And although he questioned its theological foundations, Daniel had to admit that the church had had a considerable effect on him. He attended both school and church in this building, and his educational foundations were laid here. It was probably impossible for him ever to measure the effect that the classes, services, readings, sermons, music and rituals had had on his life.

It occurred to him for the first time that the birth of the man they were celebrating, and the church inspired by it, had in fact profoundly affected his life. Christmas, he thought, should make him grateful if nothing else.

The service progressed through a sequence of carols and readings, and it gradually gained in momentum and spirit. As they became accustomed to each other's voices the harmony of the singing improved. The preacher, whatever his earlier theological failings, seemed determined to show them that he still had some religion in him.

They rose to sing "As with gladness men of old...", his mother's favourite carol. Daniel listened to the gusto with which she sang. His thoughts went back to her in her lighted room in the mornings, and he thought of the strength she had drawn from the tradition which the church represented.

That strength, since his father's death when he was seven, had also sustained him. In spite of his doubts about it, he could not deny that he had benefited from his mother's religion. And so he joined in the singing of what, for him, was a carol of thanksgiving.

The time came for the sermon, and Daniel was surprised to hear the preacher inviting him to deliver the message.

The stranger and the shopkeeper turned to greet him; they had not recognized him before, and they seemed pleased at the prospect of hearing a sermon from him.

Daniel heard the preacher describing him as a child of the church, and a son of the village who had risen to a good position as a lecturer in physics. He felt their expectation focused on him, and he knew he could not disappoint them. As he started to rise from his seat he heard a soft, happy chuckle from his mother. He walked towards the lamp.

"We are assembled here," he said, "to commemorate an event which, it is believed, occurred nearly two thousand years ago. If it was in fact the event which tradition tells us it was, then it was the most important event in human history.

"But was it really what they say it was? Surely the world is as horrible a place now as it was then. So where is the peace on earth? Where is the salvation of mankind? Isn't the so-called second coming only another hope, a put-off, since the first one obviously didn't deliver the expected goods?

"As far as we know, Jesus of Nazareth wrote no books, painted no famous pictures, composed no great music, made no great discoveries or inventions, and won no military victories. Yet thousands of these things have been dedicated to his glory.

"Many claim they have been saved or redeemed by him. Yet we know very well that the behavior of many of them is as appalling, and sometimes even worse than that of the rest of us. So what are we to make of this?

"Yet when I look on this building and consider its good effects on so many, it seems clear that this religion brought a lot of good into the world. It brought a lot of evil too, mind you, like the Crusades and the Inquisition. But one cannot help being moved by the good deeds of so many missionaries and martyrs, including those who built this place in this remote rural community. And the commitment of this small band of worshippers here this morning, is testimony of the determination of those who hold this faith.

"Some are inspired by stories of miracles, and of promises of paradise after death. But for me, the most inspiring of all is the doctrine of love advocated by the man whose birth we are celebrating today. Is it a practicable doctrine? I sometimes wonder. One wit said the trouble with it is that it has never been tried. But practicable or not, it is certainly an inspiring ideal. And since you have asked me to speak to you, this is the most I can say to you. Remember the doctrine of love, and have a Merry Christmas."

Daniel walked back to his seat hoping he had managed to strike a balance between skepticism and inspiration. The few approving murmurs he heard as he sat down, and the preacher's words of appreciation suggested that his short message had been well received.

The light of morning was now in the church. As they sang the final carol, Daniel looked around on his fellow worshippers. In the soft morning light, it looked as if they were in a painting by one of the island's primitive artists: a study of a choir of country faces singing out of the life of remote hills.

After the benediction, with the light of sunrise streaming into the church, the caretaker strode through the vestry door carrying a brilliantly shining gas lamp. The people laughed, and a few of them patted him on the back and wished him Merry Christmas. Daniel looked at his mother, seeing her now in broad daylight. And in the look of satisfaction in her eyes, he saw a Christmas even deeper than his own.

The Returnee

For most of his life, Vincent was a typical Jamaican homophobe. As a small boy he overheard a man in his district telling some other men about a Chinese grocer in a neighbouring district who paid black men for sex. He was shocked and horrified by the behaviour of this Chinese grocer and his black accomplices. One Saturday night there was a dance in the district, and Vincent joined a group of onlookers at the back of the shop as they stood and watched the dancers enjoying themselves in the booth.

One of the men who stood with them — perhaps the same one who was telling people about the Chinese grocer — identified one of the dancers, a brown man in his early twenties who wore ill-fitting trousers, as a b-man. It was his first time hearing the word, but he inferred that it was the name for people like the Chinese grocer. The young man was having a good time dancing with a woman, and the name applied to him was of course only a rumour, but immediately it made him something of a monster in Vincent's mind.

Throughout his schooldays and young adulthood he would from time to time hear this word applied to men he knew, always in their absence. It was applied to an older man of unknown occupation who often hung out with the boys on the wall at the end of the square. It was applied to a scoutmaster who also liked hanging out with boys. It was applied to the articulate and aloof college student who played tennis.

By the time he reached adulthood, he knew that it was the most derogatory word in the Jamaican lexicon, perhaps even worse than 'murderer' or 'atheist'. But he never had any close, personal contact with any of the persons so labelled. In time he came to know that the English word 'homosexual' meant the same as the Jamaican 'b-man'. Interestingly, he never heard the word homosexual applied to a woman. He heard all these rumours and believed them without question. It never occurred to him that these allegations could be false, mistaken or malicious.

After completing his B.A. in history on the island, he taught this subject at a high school in Kingston for three years. Then he obtained a scholarship to read for a master's degree in sociology in Toronto, Canada. Shortly after arriving there, he spent a weekend with a Jamaican migrant family he had known from back home. After supper one evening the husband announced that he would boil some corn on the cob, and he bragged about his skill in doing this, using butter, peppers and other seasonings. He was the principal of an elementary school, and he said that his deputy, a homosexual, would soon be joining them to enjoy some of the corn. This bit of information disturbed Vincent very much, for he did not want to socialize with or even see such a person.

So he made up an excuse that he had an essay to

write and went upstairs to his room. He mounted the steps in great haste as he tried to escape the homosexual. He read in bed and then went to sleep. He had an erotic dream in which he was making love to a white woman his friends had introduced him to earlier that day. Back on the campus, he saw a poster on one of the bulletin boards advertising a "Gay Concert", and since to him the word 'gay' meant 'happy and cheerful', he thought it might be fun to go.

He told a Canadian acquaintance about the poster, and in response the man limped his wrist, made some effeminate movements and explained what the word 'gay' now meant. That was a close shave! thought Vincent. During Orientation Week, the clubs and societies had their booths in the Students' Union Building. He toured them as he tried to decide which one to join.

He was shocked when he came upon a gay booth being manned, or womanned, by real live homosexuals. He was afraid to even look at them, so he hurried by while looking the other way. One evening while walking in one of the gardens on the campus, he saw two young women on a bench openly hugging and kissing each other, oblivious to him, a shocked Jamaican passerby. Even before classes began it was clear to him that this country had a different attitude to homosexuals.

He shared a house with two Canadian graduate students. Ron, a medical student, was a dark-haired giant who stood over six feet and had a body that was broader than that of two ordinary men. Larry, who was studying film, was of medium height, and had dark-brown hair with sideburns and a beard; one noticed his gentle blue eyes. Each of them had his own room, and they shared a bathroom, kitchen, lounge and telephone. They took turns putting out the garbage.

One day he returned home for lunch and found his two housemates already at the table having theirs. He joined them with his cheese sandwich and orange juice. Ron, on his left, was having chilli and rice, and Larry who sat facing him, was enjoying a bowl of soup. They were discussing a big hit song, and Larry announced that most members of the group were gay. He proceeded to describe the gay lifestyle and culture in San Francisco, and seemed very informed. He began getting into what Vincent regarded as very sordid details.

"Disgusting!" exclaimed Vincent.

"You've insulted me and all gay people!" declared Larry, his face red with rage.

"I wasn't being personal," said Vincent. "Are you gay? I didn't know you are gay."

Larry began to roll out the list of what he said were acts of atrocities against gays, from the Inquisition through Hitler down to the present time. He and Vincent glared at each other with a charged animosity that was at the very brink of violence. Ron kept his eyes on his plate. Ron and Vincent hurried to finish eating, while Larry continued to rant. Vincent finished first and went to his room.

The discovery that he was living under the same roof with a man of that kind disturbed Vincent deeply. A few things started falling into place. Ron had very little spare time, but they sometimes talked about their weekends, the parties, the girls they met and so on. Larry only spoke about movies, which he insisted on calling films, but he never mentioned his social life. Vincent soon discovered that the young man who spent weekends with him sometimes was in fact his lover. He was appalled that those Sodom and Gommorah activities were going on only a few yards from his room. He expected the fire and brimstone to fall on the house at any minute. He thought of leaving, but he knew it would be difficult finding student accommodation elsewhere; the present arrangement had come about after quite a struggle.

Vincent was hoping to make the university swimming team and trained in the Aquatic Centre every evening. He wanted to prove to them that black men could swim. Before doing his laps he was loosening up in the shallow end, and noticed that Larry was in the water too. It seemed he was unable to swim and was practising putting his face in the water. Vincent noticed that the lifeguard was keeping a close eye on him.

As Vincent watched the homosexual in the water, he thought that with his activities he must be contaminating the pool. Why did they let him in? he wondered. Then it occurred to him that the white people were probably thinking the same thing about him and his black skin. After his swim he began walking towards the library, and he noticed that Larry had fallen in step with him. They engaged in polite conversation about nothing in particular, but Vincent did not like the idea of being seen walking and talking with Larry. People might think that they were of the same kind.

Larry joined Vincent at the table one morning while he was sipping coffee after his breakfast. He put a large scrapbook on the table.

"These are newspaper clippings about my activities," he said. "I am a fairly well-known gay rights activist."

He began flipping the pages and commenting on the pieces. They were from newspapers all over the country. Vincent decided he would just let him talk. "Every man has a story," his father was fond of telling him, "and you should hear what he has to say."

"I knew I was gay from I was about four years old," said Larry. "Some Indian tribes regard gay people as holy. So your attitude is not as universal as you may think. And every day you interact with gay people without knowing it. Your dentist, your mechanic or your favourite store clerk might be gay. And how can you be against racial discrimination but approve of discrimination against gay people?"

Vincent asked no questions and made no comments. He let Larry talk and when it was time for him to leave for a class he asked to be excused and left. But some of the things Larry had said made him think. He regarded homosexual activities as a form of perverse wickedness deliberately chosen by monstrous and very evil people.

But if Larry knew he was gay from he was four years old, could it be that some people were born with that disposition? Or acquired it through some strange, warped psychological process? As a student of sociology, he inclined to the view that most human behaviour was shaped by the environment: parents, family, culture, and so on. He was aware that moral values varied from culture to culture, although he also believed that there were some fundamental ones shared by all societies.

So, if true, he could buy the story about the Indians, even if he could not understand their reasoning. But these concealed gays all around made him uneasy. He did not like the idea of a gay dentist putting his hand in his mouth, or a gay doctor giving him a physical examination. So it was probably better if they came out so you knew which ones to avoid. He could think of no ready explanation of why he regarded racism as morally wrong and homophobia as morally right. One just felt wrong and the other right. He needed to think about that some more.

Vincent began adjusting somewhat to Larry's presence in the house. But he got a creepy feeling each time he saw him, and the outrage he felt at the occasional presence of his lover in his room never diminished. But sometimes he reflected on the fact that they had got on reasonably well before Larry's revelation.

He had even enjoyed some of Larry's learned analyses of films both of them had seen. Larry was required to study some sociology, and Vincent sometimes loaned him books and articles. Vincent sometimes relaxed by playing his guitar in the lounge. Along with becoming a university lecturer in sociology, his other big aim was to become a successful songwriter. He believed that the greatest gift anyone could have was the ability to compose music.

From time to time Larry would stop to listen. He asked for Jamaican songs and Vincent would play some Bob Marley and Don Drummond. But Larry would ask for Harry Belafonte. Larry was interested in the fact that Vincent was an aspiring songwriter who found songwriting even more interesting and satisfying than performing. Vincent explained that Jamaicans were known to admire performers, but had very little interest in the people who composed the music. Unlike the United States which had awards for songwriters, the songwriter was a very shadowy figure in Jamaican music. Few people knew anything about them or even cared to know who they were, how they worked, and what their accomplishments were. He believed it had something to do with an absence of regard for the creativity of the individual in the country's history and culture.

To help remedy this he was researching a book on famous Jamaican songs and the stories behind them.

Vincent had enjoyed these discussions. So why should Larry's revelation about his sexuality transform him so drastically in his mind? In all other respects he was the same person. And since Larry's sexual proclivities did not concern him on a personal level, why should he care about them? He was no threat to him personally. One day, as their co-existence was becoming more civil, Larry shocked Vincent with the following question:

"Do you think there might be a job for me at your Jamaican university?" he asked while they were at the table having supper. "I would love to work there. It sounds like such a beautiful place."

"I would advise you to stay clear of that island," said Vincent. "I have read of mob attacks on suspected gays there. Someone might chop you up with a machete. Besides, I doubt that they have any film studies there."

Vincent was taking a course on philosophy of social science. One day while browsing in the philosophy section in the library he saw a big book titled *Equality*, and he took it from the shelf and looked at the table of contents. It looked interesting so he borrowed it and took it home, and read some of the articles. He discovered a few new things about the history of the concept in Western civilization.

For example he was intrigued by the role that the teachings of Jesus of Nazareth and the Enlightenment thinkers had played in the development of this moral principle in the West. While he was not outwardly religious, he came from a churchgoing family — his mother was deeply religious — and had always admired Jesus as a moral revolutionary.

This was a man who hung out with outcasts and even washed the feet of his disciples, an activity that was usually done by slaves. But he had never linked those activities with the evolution of this moral principle. Furthermore, it so happened that while he was reading one of the chapters, he saw the Canadian Prime Minister on television being interviewed about gay marriage.

When asked for its justification he had replied, "Because we believe in equality." This interview reinforced Vincent's perception that this country did in fact take this gay rights thing seriously. He recalled reading about a professor who told an anti-gay joke in his class. It insulted two gay students who asked him to withdraw it. He refused.

They reported him to the administration and he was ordered to apologise to the gay students. He again refused. He was fired. There were laws there that protected these people. It occurred to Vincent that if his conflict with Larry had become violent he would probably have been expelled from the university, and he would have been on a plane back to the island.

He began putting the book and the Prime Minister's remark together. His philosophy professor loved constructing syllogisms, so he wondered what kind of syllogism might be constructed on this issue. After a few attempts he came up with one that went like this:

1. All citizens should have equal rights.
2. Gay people are citizens.
3. Therefore gay people should have equal rights.

Looked at coldly, it seemed a reasonably good argument. His professor would say that to refute it he would have to show that either the premises are false or that the conclusion does not follow from them.

Even if he quibbled a bit with the first premise, it looked like something he could accept in principle. The second was unquestionably true. So the conclusion seemed to follow. But if the logic was as simple and clear as that, why has there been so much inequality in the world?

It seemed clear to him that if the Pope believed in this argument he would allow women priests. The Americans have this principle written in their Constitution, yet look at what they have done to black and native people. Many governments, including his own, still discriminated against gay people, and some even executed them. But he had to admit that many people, including the fired professor and himself, had very strong gut feelings against gays and their lifestyle. Suddenly it clicked in his mind that it was the moral principle of equality that was violated by both racism and homophobia.

If he substituted 'black' for 'gay' in the argument he had just constructed, it would also yield the conclusion that black people should have equal rights. But it was clear that it was not easy to apply this principle and argument in the real world. If the logic was so clear but racism and homophobia still existed, they must be based on something other than logic. But what was it? Emotions perhaps? This thing seems deeper than logic, he told himself.

All his previous relationships with women had progressed from a strong, physical, sexual attraction, to getting to know them better as persons, and culminating in a kind of gentle compassion. With Candace things moved in the opposite direction. He was first drawn to her sweet and innocent sincerity, then as he got to know her better, it flared into a torrid sexual relationship.

He met her in a cafeteria on campus. He was walking with his tray and looking for a seat when he saw Cathy, a Canadian friend from one of his courses, waving and beckoning to him to join her and her female companion at their table. As he sat down she introduced her friend Candace who had long black hair, olive complexion and large, brown, soulful eyes.

At first he thought she might be Latin American, or even Caribbean, for he knew of women in Jamaica who looked like her. But her accent did not sound as if it came from his part of the world, and he had difficulty placing it. Cathy told him that Candace had come to Canada from New Zealand, and that she was studying for her master's degree in English.

For a while they talked about one of Cathy's favourite subjects: Jamaican culture, especially its music and films. She had holidayed on the island, spent Spring Break in Negril, and had, he thought, a rather romantic view of the country. But Cathy soon had to leave for a class, and he and Candace were left to get to know each other better.

They spoke for nearly three hours. Her father was a white New Zealander and her mother was an immigrant from India. Her family had migrated to Canada while she was still in her teens, and she had completed high school and her first degree there. She had a younger sister and a brother. Sadly, her father had died shortly after they arrived in Canada.

Her mother, who was less well educated than her stockbroker father, worked as a shop assistant. She said her father had been very wise with his investments, so they owned a home and were managing fairly well. She had no idea what she would do with her life after her degree. She did not feel she was ready to do a doctorate; she was not sure she wanted to teach. With the biographical information out of the way, they launched into a long discussion about the social value of literature. He defended Marx's view that the English novel revealed more about that society than the history books did.

She talked about what her favourite authors — Joseph Conrad, Jane Austen and Henry James — had taught her about society. He noticed that her eyes would go from warm to cold, with the coldness predominating. But for some reason he regarded this coldness as a challenge. He wanted to warm her up. So when the cafeteria was about to close he asked her for her telephone number, and she wrote it on a piece of paper and handed it to him.

He was in a daze as he drove home on the subway. He had never had such a long and deep conversation with a woman on the very first meeting.

"Seems you are falling in love," said Ron after he told him about Candace over their midnight snack at the table. As lovers of women, they were bonding in their contrast with the gay man.

Vincent and Candace continued with long conversations on the telephone. He finally invited her to a movie and she consented. She suggested a women's film festival that was underway in the city, and he said that sounded very interesting for he had never experienced such a festival. She said she would pick him up since she owned a car and he didn't.

They saw several of the films. In fact it was meeting her that brought the city to life for him. They began visiting the various attractions. They were both outsiders, even if she was a little less so than he was, having been in the country longer, so they slipped comfortably into the roles of tourists, and she enjoyed being hostess and tour guide to the places she knew better. They sampled ethnic restaurants including those featuring food from New Zealand, India and Jamaica.

They visited the CN Tower, the Art Gallery of Ontario, and attended literary readings at the Harbourfront (Candace had a special interest in these and was his guide to the authors). At the St. Lawrence Market he was able to compare it with the Jamaican equivalents. She came to the Aquatic Centre and sat in the balcony to watch him train.

When he failed to make the swimming team she took him to dinner to cheer him up. She chose one of her favourite places, a Fiji-Indian restaurant where they were able to enjoy the curries they both loved, as well as cassava soup and fried plantains. One of their favourite activities was buying pastries in Chinatown and taking them back to his room to enjoy them with Jamaican coffee.

Then he would play reggae and other forms of Caribbean music, always paying special attention to his favourite songwriters like Irving Burgie and Bob Andy. She brought over her own records, and these included albums by Edith Piaf, her favourite singer. She said the experiences she heard in Piaf's music resonated very deeply with her.

But when the gentle and sweet compassion he felt flared into a strong sexual desire, she resisted him. She had kissed other men before, she said, and she hadn't enjoyed it. But some men had a kind of aura, she admitted. He appealed to her most when he wore tight designer jeans and muscle T-shirts. But even these could not get her to yield. He gave up and told her he would start dating other women, but that he valued her friendship and hoped they would remain friends.

For some reason this had a dramatic effect on her. She said no other man had ever reacted to her rejection by welcoming her friendship. And then she began chasing him with great ferocity. They hugged on the campus in the dark night and kissed for what seemed like hours. If, coming from the shower, he entered his room without a shirt on, she would rush at him and cover his chest and torso with her kisses. She was his first virgin. And no woman ever begged him more passionately to to do it harder, stronger and longer.

She invited him to have lunch with her family. She picked him up and they drove to her home in the suburbs. Her mother wore a sari and was cheerful and welcoming. She was the opposite in temperament to her late dour and scholarly husband, Candace said later. Vincent was introduced to Candace's younger sister Anne, who resembled her mother more than Candace did, and to Tom, the youngest, who appeared to be a hyperactive ten year-old. Candace's siblings then kept out of the way until lunch was served. Vincent conversed with her mother who was mostly interested in his studies and career plans.

She said Harry Belafonte's *Jamaica Farewell* was one of her favourite songs. She left to continue preparing lunch and Candace showed him some of the family photo albums. Her father looked a bit like Gary Cooper in *High Noon*. At lunch he let Anne and Tom talk about school, and he encouraged their mother to reminisce about the three countries in her life. She missed the landscapes of New Zealand.

Then she spoke a bit about the food she had served, which was mostly from southern India, the place of her birth and upbringing. Then Candace played some Maori and Indian music. After the pleasant family gathering she drove him home.

One night they were having a drink in the bar at the Graduate Students Centre. She was having her usual gin and tonic and he was having a Guinness stout. For some reason or other their conversation got around to the topic of homosexuality.

"The psychologists no longer regard it as a mental illness," said Candace.

"I believe it is a form of social learning," he said.

"I believe it is mostly biologically determined," she said. " I was reading recently about a study that found that it is more common among left-handed people than among those who are right handed. And they can't explain sidedness either, which occurs only in humans. And homosexuality exists in roughly the same percentage in all known societies.

"And it has been around for all of recorded history. Scientists have even observed it in some plants and animals. The idea of cultural variation would seem to work against findings of this kind, I think. Some are now even positing that gay men may have women's brains and lesbians have men's brains."

"Perhaps it isn't monocausal," he said. "Perhaps it is a mix of nature and nurture. Perhaps it is very complicated. Or caused by some simple thing scientists have been overlooking for centuries."

"That is quite possible."

"You seem to know quite a bit about it."

"I am interested in social outcasts," she said, smiling mysteriously. "Literature is full of them. And they tend to be more interesting than the good guys. Look at Satan in *Paradise Lost* and Ahab in *Moby Dick*."

He noticed that the people at the next table seemed to be eavesdropping on their conversation, and he mentioned it to Candace.

"I don't blame them," she said with a laugh. "It is such an interesting topic."

Vincent was thinking about some of these ideas when he had his last conversation with Larry. They met in front of the building which housed Larry's department. He was wearing some kind of costume: striped, multi-coloured shirt and pants, and a round straw hat, the kind Vincent associated with barbershop singing groups.

"We got off to a bad start," said Larry, "but at least we can be civil now."

"I will watch the film credits for your name," said Vincent.

"Director! You will see my name as a director!"

"Sure," said Vincent as he began walking away. "And I wish you the best."

Vincent and Candace completed their degrees. He knew that he had to return home when his scholarship and student visa expired. Candace could not make up her mind what she wanted to do. They were developing a hot and very intense connection, but although she was hinting at it, they both felt that they were not yet ready for marriage.

At the same time they knew that a separation in the heat of this connection would be very painful for both of them. After nights out and hours of kissing, they sometimes sat in her car for many more hours discussing what they should do; on a few occasions they talked until daylight. After reading an article on the Canadian University Service Overseas (CUSO), Vincent cut it out and showed it to Candace. He suggested that she should apply. Perhaps they would send her to Jamaica.

She applied and they offered her a teaching post at a university in Nigeria. He urged her to accept it. She finally decided that she would. He suggested that they continue being friends but keep their relationship open. But Candace wanted a firm commitment. However, he had a fear of long distance relationships, and preferred to let nature take its course. They finally agreed that she would go to Nigeria and he would return to Jamaica. She would visit him on the island the following summer.

The day he packed his suitcase Candace was in his room watching him. She had a comment on each shirt as he took it from the closet:

"You wore that one the day we went to the CN Tower," she said about the one that was blue, tapering and chequered.

"You had on that one when we went to the St. Lawrence Market," she said as he held up another blue shirt with a western cowboy look.

"And I can still see you in that one as you crossed the bridge in the Japanese Garden," she said about his orange knitted shirt.

"Shirt tales!" he said and laughed.

Candace drove him to the airport. She took a photo of him sitting in one of the chairs in the lounge. They talked about her preparations to leave for Nigeria. "This city won't look the same without you being here," she said. "Thanks for all you have made me feel and see." He squeezed her hand and kissed her lips. When the departure of his flight was announced he began walking towards the tunnel. He stopped at the entrance and turned to wave goodbye. There she was, standing alone in their city.

There was a deep sadness in his heart. He began walking towards the aircraft. He was on his way to becoming a returnee.

He got a teaching job at a small community college in one of the northern parishes. The campus and the nearby market-town were surrounded by green hills which looked like egg-cartons. There were cattle farms on the flat areas. Small farmers cultivated yams and sweet potatoes on the hillsides. There were several pimento groves. The sea was only seven miles from the campus, and there was a public beach there as well as a few small hotels and cottages.

He lived in one of the small cottages on the campus. While growing up on the island his mother wouldn't let him near the kitchen, except to break coconuts or open bottles with stiff lids, but while in Canada necessity had forced him to learn to cook. Now he tried to apply his acquired techniques to the use of local ingredients. He hired a woman to wash and clean one day per week.

Candace called from Toronto the day before she left for Nigeria. Then her letters began arriving. She too lived in a cottage on her campus. She told him scary stories about having to keep her doors always closed to prevent snakes from crawling in, and making sure to carefully iron her clothes to destroy the eggs an insect laid in them while they were on the line, otherwise the hatched creatures would bore into her skin.

He thought, gratefully, of the rather benevolent fauna of his island: there were no venomous snakes, and apart from mosquitoes and the occasional crocodile, he had little to fear from wild animals. She bought woodcarvings from a trader who said they were used in initiation rituals. She began travelling the country and sent him photographs of dramatic landscapes which sometimes looked a bit like the Caribbean. He longed to hear her voice and tried calling, but he was told there was no line to her rural university. So they began recording their messages on cassettes and mailing them to each other.

The following summer she travelled from Nigeria to Jamaica, via Toronto, to spend time with him. He saw this as evidence that she was very serious about the relationship and wanted the commitment. They drove all around the island and took many photographs. When she returned to Toronto, on her way back to Nigeria, she sent him a little photo album with a selection of these photos. Some of them became his favourites.

There was the one of both of them at Reggae Sumfest. They were leaning on the T-shaped reggae-sticks that boys sold to patrons to rest their legs. They were hoping to hear a band they had first heard on one of their dates in Toronto, but they did not come on until eight o' clock the following morning, by which time they were back at their hotel.

There was one of himself standing beside his white Toyota parked beside the cottage on the campus. It was now his turn to drive Candace around.

He was wearing one of the tapered shirts and the designer jeans that she said gave him that aura.

He liked the one of Candace standing in front of a magnificent cluster of palms up at the Bonnie View Hotel. She was wearing her signature blue jeans and pink blouse which he was so used to seeing her wear in

Toronto. The palms were radiating a warm, lush, tropical vitality.

There was one of himself emerging from the sea in Negril after a long, vigorous swim. She captured his broad shoulders and deep chest, features that seemed to fascinate her.

Another showed her against the magnificent backdrop of the view from Spur Tree Hill. The wind was playing with her hair. There was a mysterious expression on her pretty face.

Finally, there was the one that tugged at his heart the most. It was of his family home in Portland. It was a portrait of himself standing before hills he knew so well. He was framed by banana and coffee leaves. It was the only photograph that he had of himself in his home environment.

Before Candace took that photograph, he had introduced her to his mother, father, and brothers Clive and Andrew. Clive followed him and was an electrician; Andrew was still going to high school. He had no sister and so felt he was always searching for one. His mother served chicken and rice and peas with vegetables and fried plantains.

This was followed by coconut water from coconuts his father picked from a tree near the yard. Candace told them about New Zealand and her only visit to India. His father told her about life in their community when he was a boy, and she liked his story about the River Mumma and the Golden Table he claimed he had seen in the river. His mother concentrated on making them comfortable.

After dinner Vincent showed Candace around and introduced her to some of the plants, but she said she had already seen some of them in Nigeria. He joked that he did not like the way Nigeria was stealing his thunder. After a pleasant visit to the hills they said goodbye to his family and were on their way.

He had no photos of the performance of the National Dance Theatre Company that they saw at the Little Theatre, or of the Trevor Rhone play at The Pegasus Hotel. Neither did he have any of the interiors of buildings. Their long conversations in the cottage, verbal, physical and emotional, were recorded only in their memories.

At the end of the month it was time for her to return to Nigeria via Toronto. He drove her to the Montego Bay airport. After she checked in at the airline counter they sat on one of the long benches and chatted. A tourist woman who was standing in front of them pulled up her dress to scratch her thigh. He noticed that Candace responded visibly, and he felt she was uneasy about how he would respond to the woman's nudity right in front of her. When the departure of the flight was announced, they stood up and embraced each other.

"Is this the end?" asked Candace.

"No. It is only the beginning," he replied.

Vincent went up to the waving gallery and watched as she crossed the tarmac , mounted the steps and went into the aircraft. His eyes followed the plane as it taxied out for takeoff. He watched as it rose into the sky and disappeared into the clouds.

On his way home he made up his mind. As the man who had taken her virginity, he felt he was her natural husband. They got along well together. He believed she was a good woman. He felt that tender care and com-passion, and feeling of oneness with her that he defined as love. He decided he would ask her to marry him.

He waited eagerly to receive a letter from Candace but, unusually, none came. He was worried about her safety so he called her mother in Toronto. She said as far as she knew Candace was fine. She even told him she thought Candace was lucky to have a boyfriend who cared so much about her. So he wrote to Candace and told her that her long silence was causing him much concern.

In the meantime he was busy with his heavy teaching load. One of the courses he taught was Introduction to Sociology. They were examining some of the conceptions of man and the different types of men studied in sociology. One of the students raised the issue of homosexuality. A reporter on one of the newspapers had been investigating the island's homosexual underworld and publishing her findings. He had read some of them. The issue was being widely discussed.

"Sir, what causes homosexuality?" a female student asked.

"As far as I am aware it is psychologically unexplained," he replied. "There have been many theories, but so far none has been demonstrated to be true."

"But what do you think?" the student pressed.

"I used to think it was a form of social conditioning. But I now incline to the view that it has a bio-psychological origin. Scientists say they have observed it in some plants and animals. One study found that it is more common in left-handed people than in right-handed people. Another suggests that gay men may have women's brains, and lesbians men's brains."

"It is unnatural!" declared a male student at the back. His tone was very aggressive.

"Not if it turns out to have a biological origin and is caused by genes, hormones or the structure of people's brains. In that case it would be natural for some people. Natural means not caused by human beings."

"How do we know you are not one of them?" muttered a female student who was sitting right in front of him. He glared at her but ignored her.

"They should all be lined up and shot!" declared the aggressive male student.

This outburst shocked Vincent. He was aware that he was living in a violent society, but the thought passed through his mind that if a school was to change this positively it had to be better, and at least less violent, than the society in which it was embedded.

"Are you a Christian?" he asked the student.

"Yes, and the Bible condemns all sodomites!"

"This is a religious-based institution isn't it?" he said. "I thought Jesus taught love, compassion and equality for all. In fact he contributed to the development of the concept of equality in the West. His philosophy was to comfort outcasts and the downtrodden and the stigmatized. I can't imagine Jesus of Nazareth lining up gay people and shooting them. And not all societies condemn gay people. The Greeks accepted and even idealized same-sex love. One Indian tribe regards them as holy. Your attitudes are not as universal as you think."

The bell rang and they moved on to their next class. He forgot about the class discussion. He had other things on his mind. He was worried about Candace in Nigeria. There had been reports about violent clashes between Muslims and Christians resulting in many deaths.

A few nights later his telephone rang while he was having supper. It kept ringing while he tried to swallow his food. He quickly sipped some hot Milo and rose from his desk.

"B-man pick up the phone!" a female student shouted from the nearby residence.

He was shocked and horrified to hear that vile epithet applied to him. In his view it was the ugliest and most degrading word in the Jamaican lexicon, and it referred to that which was most obnoxious and abominable in human nature. The saying that sticks and stones hurt more than words was nonsense, for that word hurt him to the quick.

It was true that he was now more inclined to at least believe in tolerance for gay people, but he was one hundred percent heterosexual and had no homosexual leanings whatsoever. In a way it seemed laughable to hear himself so designated. But he could not laugh. In the days ahead he would hear the b-word uttered behind him as he passed groups of students on the campus and in the town. He heard it uttered as he passed taxi stands, and once it came from a gang of youths who were hanging around the entrance of a tax office.

Once he even heard it on a street in Kingston. It was often phrased as the "b-man sociologist". The hated word had a fierce corrosive power, and it began eating away at his mind. Then when he saw it scrawled in the dust on his car, he knew that the scandal was on its way. When he heard the word hurled at him with a great deal of contempt and hostility, as he drove through the town one day, he knew he was in trouble.

The trouble with that kind of rumour, he thought, was that there was no objective way of proving it false. As far as he was aware, there was no blood test or MRI scan that could determine a person's sexual orientation. Only the individual knew for sure. And he knew that he was a heterosexual. But could anyone else know his mind? He recalled that this was what his philosophy professor had called the problem of other minds.

At the same time no one would confront him with it directly so he could deny it. It was gathering momentum and was completely out of his control. It was growing rapidly like a horrible monster around him, powerfully negating his truth and his reality in the eyes of those who heard it. He knew that on hearing it people would believe it immediately without question and begin passing it on.

Before long it would be all over the small island for his students were everywhere. He would be a marked man. Before long his compatriots would begin perceiving and despising him as a warped and despicable creature. This illusory perception would now dominate all his other attributed characteristics, and would become the first and probably the only thing that entered the minds of other people when they saw or thought about him. He was living like a goldfish in a bowl, and his every move was now being scrutinized for further evidence of this alleged homosexuality.

He did not know about what psychologists call confirmation bias: the preference for information that seems to confirm what one wants to believe, regardless of how overwhelming the contrary evidence is. But he was experiencing it. For it seemed to him that a lot of people preferred to be hateful, and would therefore clutch at anything that appeared to give them an excuse for doing so.

Especially if it was aimed at someone perceived to be in a position of authority and privilege. They would take a savage delight in tearing him down. Shakespeare said something about festering lilies smelling worse than weeds. They wanted his reputation to stink. So in the minds of the people around him, his past girlfriends, some of whom were known to his friends and colleagues, were now thrown out the window.

If female relatives or friends visited him they were ignored. But if a male relative, friend or colleague visited him, the man was immediately dubbed a visiting homosexual. Vincent saw the evil thing expanding around him, and he soon discovered that any attempt at fighting it, by word or deed, was only likely to make it worse.

Then it occurred to him that he himself used to believe such allegations about people uncritically, so he may actually have helped to spread false rumours about innocent people. He felt a pang of remorse. He had become a victim of an attitude he himself once had. What if the Buddhist doctrine of karma or retribution was true? he began to wonder.

He became deeply afraid of the violence which might be inflicted on him. The newspaper reported on a man who lived alone, a suspected homosexual, whose house had been burned down. A lynch mob had brutally murdered a cross-dresser. There were also reports of the police having to rescue alleged homosexuals from such mobs.

He had seen a news-clip on television of a suspected gay man being brutally beaten. Even straight but supportive parents of their gay children had been reportedly murdered. When a gay rights activist was murdered, a celebrative crowd had gathered at his home and had cheered while the body, covered with stab wounds, was being taken to the hearse.

There was seldom a day when there weren't news reports of impassioned sermons by prominent clerics condemning homosexuality, and letters to the editors of the newspapers, quoting the Bible chapter and verse, citing the wrath of God that would descend on the nation if this evil was not removed from the society. A few politicians had publicly declared that they would never tolerate homosexuality in the country.

Media houses had refused to carry advertisements which urged tolerance. Hate speech or other exclusionary remarks directed at gay people were vigorously defended in the media as 'free speech'. Occasionally there were mild rumblings from the human rights groups, but these would soon be vociferously opposed and denounced by callers to the talk shows. The occasional letter or caller urging tolerance almost always came from overseas. While he could think of one or two mild exceptions, he had the impression that the local people who secretly believed in equal rights and tolerance for all citizens, so feared reprisals and other possible dangerous consequences for their lives and careers, that they simply cowered in fear and remained silent.

He was also worried about what the rumour could do to his relations with women. He loved and had always loved women and only women, but he was not promiscuous. He was always faithful to the woman he was dating. Now he feared this rumour could spoil his chances of finding that special woman he was seeking. A woman like Candace who, sadly it seemed, had stopped writing to him at this very critical point in his life.

He began to suffer terribly. Having once been a homophobe, he was deeply aware of the terrible image of him that now existed in people's minds. They were viewing him as an outcast, as the lowest kind of life, as even worse than a thief, murderer or atheist. They saw him as part of the scum of the earth, as a violation of the natural order of things. Yet he knew that all these beliefs were false, and he was aware that he was the only person in the world who was absolutely sure of it.

And for the first time he began to understand the importance of the ninth commandment: *You shall not bear false witness against your neighbour.* Yet it occurred to him that he had never heard a parson defend this commandment in a church. It was like the forgotten commandment. He had heard tons of sermons on all the others. He recalled reading somewhere that Zoroastrianism was the only religion with a specific commandment against lying. So many religious people would probably have no qualms about what they were doing. And in any case, many of them would see their religion as a source of justification for all the hatred and contempt they were pouring on him. Now it seemed to him that this ninth commandment was right up there with the commandment against murder.

Perhaps false-labelling was even worse than murder, for the murdered was dead, but the defamed had to live with the misery. He also recalled the African proverb that said that the worst thing you could do to a man was to break his name. His name was being broken and his identity was being warped in the minds of people. False-labelling created its own kind of anguish. His life was now in a deep crisis and he wondered how he would ever get out of it. Like Shelley, the poet he had read at school, he felt he had fallen on the thorns of life and he was bleeding profusely.

Then the letter arrived from Candace. It was a short note announcing the end of their relationship. She had discovered that she was a lesbian. An expatriate lesbian couple she had met in Africa had convinced her that she was one of them. She was now "madly in love" with another Canadian woman she had met there. The metaphoric blood now gushed from his body and soul.

It began to occur to him that the lesbian clues had been there in Candace all along, but since he wasn't looking for them, and not even given any thought to lesbians, he had failed to see them. Now those he had noticed, and others, began to fall into place: the very late losing of her virginity; being able to see only some kind of aura in some men; not enjoying being kissed by men; her strong resistance to sex after giving him reasons to believe she was interested; her choice of a female friend of his as the friend she liked best; her response to the nude women in the changing room at the pool; her preference for female singers; her knowledge of the subject and her expressed interest in outcasts; her sexual response to the woman raising her dress at the airport. Things like these began pouring into his mind, some probably relevant, some no doubt irrelevant. But he knew nothing about the minds of lesbians.

He began hearing the voices of people discussing him. Some accused him of this ancient biblical sin. The monstrous b-word dominated all the discussions. But a woman was always defending him, and he became accustomed to her voice. The voices cackled around him day and night as if coming up out of the earth. The discussions he heard went on in the students' residence and in the home of the neighbours. One day he saw a hunchbacked, old woman walking past the gate of the college.

That night as he lay in bed, he heard her voice denouncing him, loud and clear, near the cottage. It was the most evil voice he had ever heard. Another voice ordered him to call Marcia, a colleague who taught mathematics, and with whom he got on well. He called her but did not remember their conversation.

He heard the sounds of helicopters coming to take him back to Canada. A voice said he was such a virile man he could fuck even a lesbian to orgasm. He saw all his former girlfriends posing for a photograph. But Candace was not among them. When he asked for her, they said she was with his mother. He heard the voices of the gay community in the town discussing him. They were debating whether or not he was one of them. They decided that he was not. As he was looking at the whitish, ochre-coloured earth, he felt the presence of God and experienced a deep ecstasy. He began to weep into the darkness.

Marcia told him what happened afterwards. After their strange conversation she made several attempts at calling him back that night but he did not answer. The following morning she went to his cottage but found the door locked. She knocked but received no answer. She went to call the bursar and he used his master key and opened the door. They found him in bed in a trance. Marcia alerted the college authorities and they made some telephone calls. Marcia volunteered to drive him to the doctor. The college nurse accompanied them. He was fully conscious by the time they arrived.

"You had a psychotic break," said the doctor. "I am going to send you to the hospital."

The doctor said he would turn down the voices with medication. For the first time Vincent realized that many of the voices he had been hearing were really hallucinations. They were dictatorial phenomena coming from he knew not where, but entering his inner solitary self and, as he would discover, reshaping his life-story. As soon as he was admitted to the hospital he was given the medication. After a few days the voices began to diminish. Marcia and some of his other colleagues visited him. Ten days later he was discharged, and Marcia drove him to his family home in the hills of Portland.

"You are sick," said his mother as she looked into his eyes. She was a dark-skinned woman who wore a blue head-tie; he could feel her eyes searching him thoroughly and compassionately. He told her he'd had a nervous break-down.

His mother fed and nursed him. The medications had terrible side effects: they impaired his walking and made him restless. Sometimes he felt as if his brain had seized up. But when he felt a little stronger he began going down to the river to bathe in the cool, crystal water. He spent hours just looking at the hills and mountains, especially up at the Blue Mountain Peak which he had climbed several times. It was fairly quiet up in the hills with the fresh air and the birds. Gradually he felt his vitality returning.

One day Marcia came to visit him. She brought a letter from the Chairman of the Board of Governors approving his six weeks of leave. He looked at her gratefully as she sat in the easy chair facing him. She was wearing green pants and a blouse of a lighter blue-green colour. She was of medium height, full breasted, and had a beautiful complexion which always reminded him of sweetcups. She had her hair in a ponytail, and she was looking at him with the caring eyes which he knew were also easily lit by laughter.

"Are you reading?" she asked him.

"Not very much. I find it hard to concentrate. But I listen to the radio and watch a little television in the evenings."

"I brought you some crossword puzzles," she said, handing him the brown paper-bag she had been holding in her lap.

"Thanks."

"Plans are well underway for the fair at the college. But don't think about that place too much. I am a city girl, but it is beautiful up here. Just the place for you at this time, I think."

It was near Easter and his mother served them bun and cheese and glasses of soursop juice. His father, a big, strapping, dark-skinned man who wore a cloth cap, and who had been working on his farm, joined them for his snack and a short chat.

"Since him turn big man, this is the longest time he ever spent up here," he said to Marcia.

"And the time will fly by quickly," said Marcia. "In no time he will be back at work."

Marcia couldn't spend a long time for she had college work to do. She said goodbye to his parents and he walked her to her car.

"Even though I have seen only a little of them, your parents seem to have a very mellow relationship," she said.

"Yes, they've been married nearly thirty years."

"Keep bathing in that river!" she said, giving him her pretty smile. Then she drove off.

Back in the house his mother quizzed him about Marcia.

"You say she is a teacher?"

"Yes."

"That is a good profession. And she seems like a nice lady."

On one of his visits the doctor handed him a booklet titled *Schizophrenia*. That was his way of telling him what he thought the illness was. Vincent looked at the dreaded word and felt only a desire to dismiss it. How could that be? he asked himself. He knew little about this or any other mental illness and did not know anyone who suffered from any of them. It had never occurred to him that he could suffer from such a disease. He glanced at the booklet and saw that it said encouraging things. He could still have a fulfilling life and it was all right to get married. But he did not want to think about that strange and forbidding word right now. He just wanted to concentrate on feeling better.

Back at the college he resumed his duties quietly. He kept a low profile and found himself becoming more and more withdrawn. On the day of the fair, the college cafeteria served no meals. He looked at a few of the stalls but felt a desire to get away from it all. So he returned to the cottage and sat in the living room. The place seemed dark and gloomy. He was getting hungry but remembered that he had done no shopping for food. He sat there trying to decide what to do. There was a knock on the door. He opened it and saw Marcia standing there, carefully holding something wrapped in aluminium foil.

"I brought you some lunch," she said.

"Bless you, Marcia."

She had brought a cheese sandwich and a corn on the cob. He sat there quietly and ate it like a sacrament.

Vincent and Marcia were now married. They lived in a rented house on the outskirts of the town, and they were saving to buy a home of their own. They both intended to continue their careers in education. Vincent thought that one day he may even consider pursuing a PhD in sociology, and perhaps write a thesis on the ideological and social roots of homophobia on the island.

In the evenings after supper, he often sat on the verandah in the dark and played his guitar. Sometimes he could feel the sea breeze coming up from the coast and cooling his body. On one of these evenings, after he felt satisfied with the music he had just played, he put the guitar on the floor beside him, leaned back in the chair and sank into reverie. The thoughts began pouring out of his mind:

That research article I read the other day said that about half the persons labelled as homosexuals are in fact straight, and they suffer the same health consequences as the persecuted gay people. Perhaps even more so. Lies worse than sores, as the proverb says. You don't have to be gay to be a victim of homophobia. That is one thing I now know for a fact.

Yet few people are interested in people like us. I wonder how many of us are in the world? How many are there on this island? And it seems as if all of this is largely because I am a returnee. My doctor says people here often regard men who go overseas and return, as homosexuals. So with that already in their minds, and my stressing facts and moral principles, instead of quoting the Bible, was like striking a match at a gas station. What a miscalculation that was!

And they not only see male returnees as homosexuals, they also see them as madmen. And perhaps the first can cause the second, as in my case. A false belief can lead to a real illness. But little by little I am coming to understand my illness. It is not the double personality that Hollywood films make it out to be.

My doctor says it is not yet fully understood, but many scientists believe it is a form of dreaming, that I dreamt I heard voices while being awake, and that it is the result of a chemical imbalance in the brain which can be hereditary or spontaneous, and which is aggravated by stressful experiences. If I keep taking the medication to maintain the chemical balance, he says I can live a normal and fruitful life. When he heard that I am a songwriter and that I play the guitar, he told me that great composers like Beethoven and Schuman, and our own Don Drummond, suffered from mental illness, and that it is believed that the secrets of creativity may actually be in my disease.

So I could be carrying the answer to one of the biggest secrets in science in my head. Nevertheless, I now know what it is like to suffer from double stigmatization, to be in a kind of social death, as the sociologists might say. And now as a sick man I have to be appealing to the same principle of equality I was appealing to for the gays. Is Canada mash me up. It looks as if it put a split between my feelings and my thoughts.

My feelings still tell me that homosexual acts are obnoxious, but my intellect tells me that it is wrong to discriminate against and persecute the people who may engage in them. I say 'may', because not all of them engage in these illegal acts. And then Jamaica, where the negative feelings about them predominate to a horrific extent, just finished me off. But the illness has not affected my intellect. I will be following the scientific research on the formation of sexual orientation with interest. It is not easy doing that here.

A scholar who reportedly tried giving some scientific facts about homosexuality to a church group was booed, shouted down and forced to leave the platform. The speaker who followed him said homosexuality was a form of demonism, and he was given a standing ovation. My philosophy professor said you can't logically derive values from facts, so science can never tell us if homosexual acts, or any other kinds of acts, are morally right or wrong. As Einstein put it, no scientific facts about the universe can logically entail any of the moral rules in the Ten Commandments. I do not know if this is true. But I think that logic or no logic, a scientific fact should have some bearing on our moral beliefs.

If sexual orientation turns out to be a mere luck of the genetic draw, like being left–handed, which the Bible is also against, should the lucky oppress and persecute the unlucky? Is the 'luck' of my heterosexuality an earned merit which justifies my hatred and persecution of the 'unlucky' ones like Candace and Larry? My anger towards Candace has subsided quite a bit. In her relationship with me she was trying to be somebody she wasn't. In my letter to her I told her to be true to herself, as Shakespeare says, and she cannot then be false to anyone. By being false to herself she hurt me badly, for that is one way in which these gay people can certainly harm straight people like me.

I told Marcia all about Candace. She wanted me to destroy all the photographs, but I insisted on keeping the one of myself in the hills of Portland, for it is the only photo I have of myself at my home. Illness has meaning, someone says, and I am still struggling with this. Is it divine punishment for being unbiblical, as the Christians would probably say? I remain convinced that my position is Christ-like, even if paradoxically, the churchmen regard it as unChristian.

Is it my share of the inevitable suffering which the Buddha sees as the lot of all sentient beings, including the nonhuman animals? Men and beasts alike cannot escape innocent suffering. And no one escapes suffering, not kings, popes or billionaires. So is this suffering meaningless? Is it my challenge to try to be virtuous in spite of all distress, as Marcus Aurelius, whom I admire so much, urges us to do? Perhaps it is a bit of all, but most of all I see it as my share of the experience of Job in the Bible. This is the one that seems to say it all. Like him I had something like a mystical experience while at the rock-bottom of my suffering.

I saw the dry, ochre-coloured earth, felt the presence of God, and began weeping. I am still trying to make sense of it. What does it mean? Like him I see no clear definite answer, except that moment of ecstasy in the suffering which came like a kind of light, which I am still trying to interpret. Marcia is now the biggest joy in my life. It is wonderful sharing with her. She is also a member of a folksinging group, and she is the first to sing the songs I compose.

I now think of her voice as that of the woman who loves me whom I kept hearing throughout my trauma. It is time I get back to the new song I am composing. Some-one I read somewhere said the creation of art can help to heal the wounds of the spirit. If David's music could help to heal Saul it can help to heal me too.

Vincent picked up his guitar and played a few chords. He felt the salty sea-breeze cooling his body. He sang the first two lines of his emerging song: *The water of the river in my hills/ will wash away most of the pain...*

Baba

received a letter from my mother informing me that my father was not well, so I decided to go home as soon as I could. Since my car was in the shop I decided to go by minibus. I hadn't been on one in years. They have a reputation for dangerous driving, overcrowding, and interminable stopping to pick up passengers, so I approached a ride on one with some trepidation. Still, it might be a bit of an adventure, I thought. The next day was Friday, so right after teaching my last class for the day I took a bus to downtown Kingston.

As I was walking towards the depot, a young man in braids, jeans and sneakers came towards me. "Montego Bay! Mandeville! Ochie!" he called out. "Weh you a go, bredda?" he inquired as he threw both arms open in a questioning gesture. I told him my destination. "Then come quick, nuh man! A van pulling out right now!" He reached for my travelling bag but I tightened my grip on it. He led me briskly through the throng of people.

"Boss, see another one yah," he said to a tall man in dark glasses who was leaning against one of the columns. In spite of the dark glasses he seemed vaguely familiar, and was probably someone I had seen in a neighbouring community while growing up. He said nothing to the hustler, but nodded me towards the minibus which was parked beside him. The door was open so I stepped inside.

I sat beside a middle-aged woman in a blue dress who was staring dreamily through the window. She turned to me with a gold-toothed smile, and then bent her head to read the copy of *The Star* which she had on her lap. I glanced around but saw no familiar faces. I noticed that, as usual, the prettiest girl was sitting in the seat next to the driver's. This one was a browning with reddish hair.

I had left my district in my teens, and now returned mostly to visit my parents. The van's terminus was only about twenty miles into the interior of the island, about a mile beyond my district, but I knew that it would be a slow journey there.

The conductor, whom everyone called 'Ductor', arrived. He was eating a patty from a small, brown paperbag, and sipping a box-juice with a straw. As soon as the hustler brought new passengers he directed them to their seats. When the van was about three-quarters full, the driver took his seat.

The hustler hurried to his window and collected payment. Then we set off. Ductor allowed the vehicle to drive for a few moments before hopping in.

"Then is run you going to run after the van all the way?" asked an East Indian woman who was sitting near to him. "You may as well just keep running behind the van!"

"Rest yuhself!" replied Ductor hotly.

The van meandered through the streets as it kept picking up passengers. Like a magician pulling rabbits out of a hat, Ductor kept producing little artificial seats to fit into the spaces; his ingenuity would have amazed the designers of the vehicle.

"Stop overcrowding the bus!" demanded a woman behind me. "This is not a slave ship!"

"Quiet yuhself!" replied Ductor. "Everybody want to reach home."

"I love the subways in New York!" said a woman with an imitation American accent. "You get one every few minutes. When I got there I said, 'Thank God for Jesus!'"

"So why you didn't stay there?" demanded a young man in a baseball cap and jeans who sat near to me. "Oonu people who travel always gwaan like oonu better than we."

"Don't misunderstand me," said the Jamerican. "Nowhere nuh better than yard. But is politics and bad-mind people mashing up this country."

"You Jamaicans always fighting against each other," said the man who sat in the window seat beside the pretty girl; he had a foreign accent.

"Where you from?" asked the driver.

"Nigeria."

"You ever been to Ethiopia?" continued the driver. "That is the Rasta country."

"No," replied the Nigerian, "but it is my fellow African country. I am a Pan-Africanist. And Jamaica is an African country too."

The van stopped to pick up a Chinese man. "Sit here, Mr. Chin," said Ductor as he produced another of his mobile seats.

"My name is not Chin," said the new passenger with much irritation. "My name is Chang, Julius Chang!"

"Same difference," said Ductor as he chuckled at what he thought was his own wit.

"I know how you feel, Miss American Lady," said a man in the back seat. "I spent forty years in England,

and I admired their discipline and courtesy. My love for this island was my downfall. I sent back money to my relatives to buy land and build a house for me. But they did everything in their own name. When I retired and came back they threw me out. I am now homeless. Is a friend I am living with."

There were moans of anger and sympathy in the van.

"Say wha?" exclaimed the young man in the baseball cap. "Dat is wickedness!"

"Then my wife left me," continued the returning resident. "And I have diabetes and high blood pressure."

"You need a bath!" declared the woman beside me. "Go see Baba."

"I have heard of him," said the man from England. "You really think he can help me?"

"Is him help me," said my neighbour.

"Pray to Yeshua instead of Jesus," suggested a man who was speaking for the first time. "That is the mistake many people make. If you call him by the wrong name he won't answer your prayers. Ever since I start calling him by his right name things going good for me."

"I don't say his name is not important," countered my neighbour, "for in the beginning was the word and the word was God. But I don't have any experience with that. My experience was with Baba."

"Tell me more about Baba," I said to her. "I grew up hearing his drums coming across the hills, and I have heard people talk about him."

"I believe in Captain Baba," she replied. "I am an Anglican, and like most of us I used to look down on those poor, noisy Poco people until I had a bad feeling that wouldn't go away. Doctor after doctor after doctor. So I decided to try Baba. I spent a day at his mission house.

In the morning he talked to me and asked me about my dreams, and gave me a reading. He prescribed a bath.

"That night I paid my fee, lit a candle, tramped and laboured around the table, going clockwise, listening to the drumming and singing. Captain Baba led us dressed in his turban and long white robe. I tramp and sweat, tramp and sweat. Until I felt the spirit and began cooing like a peadove. The bad feeling left me. And I am fine until this day."

"I don't really believe in this magic thing," said the young man.

"There is good and bad magic," said the Nigerian. "Good magic serves the supernatural and the sacred. Bad magic harms people. Your Baba seems to deal with good magic. It is interesting that you call him Baba, for in the Yoruba language a babalawo is a healer."

"I didn't know that," said my neighbour.

We were soon in the countryside. Through the windows of the van I had glimpses of mountains and valleys. I recognized the towns and villages we were passing through. We were picking up fewer passengers now, and some were starting to disembark. The minibus became silent, until the driver put on a dancehall cassette with the foulest lyrics I had ever heard.

"Take it off! Take it off!" yelled my neighbour. "There are decent people in this van!"

"Back it up, driver, back it up!" urged the young man.

"John Crows will soon be flying over this van!" said a woman.

"Driving on this dangerous road, we should be singing and praying," declared my neighbour. "Not listening to devil music!"

The driver relented and put on a gospel cassette. A woman began singing along and was soon joined by others.

We were now going downhill, with the driver skillfully negotiating the corners. There was no more conversation for a long time. The van was like a music recital on wheels.

"My stop is coming up," said my neighbour, about half-an-hour later.

"Nice meeting you," I said, "and thanks for telling us about Baba."

"What is your name?" she said as she examined me carefully.

"Luke Rhoden."

"I am Sandra Mulligan. What do you do?"

"I teach history."

"I could never remember the dates."

"It is more important to remember the periods and the events. Only a few dates are crucial."

"One stop, driver!" she called out. The minibus pulled up in front of a small shop. I rose to give her space to disembark. Then I moved over to enjoy the view from the window.

We were soon driving alongside a river. I looked at the huge boulders, some of which were probably lying there long before the arrival of the ancestors of those of us in the minibus. I watched the running water, in its never-ending journey to the sea; I knew it would eventually rise up to the sky, and perhaps eventually return to the river.

With the gospel music in the background, I observed the changing landscapes, seeing more than I would have noticed had I been driving. I looked at the houses and contemplated a thesis on the history of vernacular architecture if I ever got to university. I enjoyed the beauty of the countryside and daydreamed, until it was my time to shout, "One stop, driver!" I got out of the vehicle and went to the driver's window and paid him. The van drove off, and I began walking along the road, enjoying the renewed activity of my legs as I walked on familiar earth, going home.

My father said he was feeling better, and, like many Jamaican men, was reluctant to go to the doctor. He believed there was nothing that some white rum and lime juice could not cure. But I managed to persuade him that as soon as I got back my car, I would return to take him to the doctor.

With my car serviced and running well, I returned as soon as I could. We awoke early, and my mother served us fried eggs, hard-dough bread and mint tea. We set off while the mist was still settled in the valleys, and the air was fresh and sweet. I had to turn on my windscreen wiper to remove the dew. We travelled in silence. The doctor was in the nearest town eight miles away.

When we arrived, the doctor's white BMW was already parked in front of his office. He was there on weekday mornings, and it was said that he spent the afternoons with his race horses. I parked my car beside his, and we came out and went up the steps. The waiting room was nearly full of patients. We registered with the doctor's wife, who was small, light-skinned, and had sharp features. She was also the receptionist and nurse. After registering we were told to sit down and wait for my father's name to be called.

The patients, who were mostly women, were all very well dressed. The women wore hats and long dresses, and the men felt hats and trousers made of heavy material. There were two or three children running around, and who were continually being called back to their parents or guardians.

The walls were bare, and quite unlike those of my own doctor in the city, who had covered his walls with prints of tortured self-portraits by Vincent van Gogh. There was no coffee table with magazines, perhaps because it was believed that the country people would either be unable or uninterested in reading them. All attention was focused on the receptionist and on the names she called. Each time she pulled a docket from the stack on her desk, she called the name, and then accompanied the patient to the doctor's office.

"Cyril Nelson!" she called out about forty-five minutes later.

A stout woman in a black-and-white polka-dot dress began helping the man beside her to his feet. The man rose slowly, and with the help of a walking stick, and with the assistance of the woman, began walking towards the doctor's office. The receptionist rose and escorted them inside. Then she came out and closed the door.

"You know who that is?" asked my father.

"No."

"Baba."

"Really!"

"He heals others, himself he cannot heal," said my father who was not normally a scripture-quoting man.

"The physician cannot heal himself," I said, continuing the biblical mode. "Even doctors have to visit other doctors. Still, it is a bit surprising seeing him here. I wonder if faith healers visit other faith healers too?"

About fifteen minutes later, Cyril Nelson, AKA Baba, emerged from the doctor's office, being gently guided by his chaperone who had her right arm round his waist. He was of above average height, sepia-complexioned, and wore a brown felt hat, white long-sleeved shirt, and grey pants.

His eyes were very bright, but their lustre could not conceal his pain. The chaperone paid the bill in cash.

Then, with his right elbow in her palm, she began guiding him towards the door. They passed only inches in front of us, this man who was reputed to have healed hundreds of people. I was reminded of the woman in the Bible who obeyed her urge to touch the hem of Jesus' garment. Very slowly, they went through the door.

With my father's visit to the doctor completed, we went next door to the pharmacy to fill the prescription. It was a long wait, and it was after mid-day before I had the medication in my hand. My mother would have lunch waiting for us, but we were both hungry, and the doctor had advised my father against having an empty stomach for long periods. So we went into the nearest restaurant. I bought patties for both of us, an egg-nog for my father and an orange juice for myself. I also bought patties for my mother; it was one of her favourite foods. My father and I sat at a table and began eating.

"Tell me what you know about Baba," I said to him.

"People from all over the island go to him. You should see the big cars that park beside his mission house nearly everyday. Politicians, businessmen, civil servants. Many people don't make a single important decision before consulting him. And he helps the local people a lot, especially women and children. He is a bachelor. Says he is married to the Spirit."

"Have you ever been to see him?"

"No, but I know people who swear by him."

"I am curious about that getting into the spirit and speaking in unknown tongues. Some psychologists say the rhythmic jumping can induce that state. A friend of mine who teaches physical education was teaching her students one of the Jamaican dances, and one of the girls got into the spirit. She was scared out of her wits and decided she would stop teaching those dances. She says she is a Christian woman."

"You don't believe in the spirit world?" His tone suggested that he did.

"I don't know what to believe. And the talking in tongues. I heard of a Jew who said he heard them speaking Hebrew! I wonder what the psycholinguists have to say about that."

"The who?"

"The people who study language and the mind."

"You study that high?"

"I study history, not linguistics."

"Well, don't study too high me boy, or you may have to go to see Baba."

"I hope he gets better," I said.

With lunch over we got into the car and drove home.

A few weeks later I was back in the district to see how my father was doing. This time I was accompanied by my wife Rose and my five year-old daughter Roselee. I felt that a weekend in the country would be a nice break from the apartment in the city. My father was doing better, but complaining about the new-fangled tablets which had replaced the good, old-time bottled medicine. He was never one to complain about food, and was submitting to the diet the doctor had prescribed, and which my mother was following to the letter.

On the Saturday evening I decided to go to the local bar to have a drink with the men. It was one of my ways of keeping in touch with my community. The scholars say education alienates West Indians from their communities, and I was trying to prevent that from happening to me. I found three men in the bar: Alfie, the bus driver, was leaning against the counter on the right; he was of a taut, muscular build, of dark-brown complexion, and he was wearing a floral shirt and blue trousers. His bus had arrived from the city only a short while before, and was parked at the other end of the square.

Beside him, and sitting on a stool in the middle, was Maas Dan the mason, whom most people called Finzi; he was dark-skinned and had a round, affable face, and was wearing a blue-and-white check shirt and navy blue trousers. Beside him in the left corner, and leaning against the counter, was Rufus who doubled as a farmer and tax collector; he was tall and light-skinned and always wore fashionable haircuts.

"Gentlemen!" I said as I entered.

"Is only one gentleman in here," said Maas Dan turning to me. "And that is Rufus. The rest of us are vagabonds and ruffians."

"Speak for yourself, Finzi," said Alfie.

"Where is Denny?" asked Maas Dan. "Why you didn't bring him with you?"

"The doctor took him off alcohol," I said.

"We know another doctor we could recommend," said Maas Dan.

We all laughed. I explained that my father was also off sweet drinks. And a glass of water was not strong enough to pull him to the bar. "I left him watching horseracing on TV," I continued. "My mother and Rose are in the kitchen teaching my daughter how to make coconut cakes. He won't be able to enjoy those either."

"Old age is a bitch me boy," said Maas Dan.

I greeted Miss Imogene, the short, smiling barmaid, and after our usual courtesies I ordered a round of drinks. Maas Dan stuck with his white rum and water; Rufus ordered a Red Stripe; Alfie a milk and stout; and I had my usual Guinness stout. We began discussing recent events in the district and in the island. During the course of our conversation someone mentioned Baba's funeral.

"Funeral!" I exclaimed. "I didn't hear that he died. I knew he was ill."

"Yes, man," said Maas Dan. "Baba is dead and buried in the Catholic cemetery."

"Catholic cemetery!" I exclaimed once more. "But he was a Revivalist."

"He converted shortly before he died," said Alfie. "He went to the Catholic church, asked for the priest, and confessed."

"Confessed!" I exclaimed again. "What did he have to confess?"

"Only he and the priest will know that," said Rufus. "I am a Catholic myself. When a man is confronting death he has to do what he thinks is right."

"I confess I am a bit shocked by this news," I said. "Revivalism came out of the Great Revival of 1860-61. African religious beliefs surfaced in it and mixed with Christian ones. Our cultural nationalists are very proud of it as a part of our African heritage, and as an example of what they call Creolization, our indigenous hybrid heritage."

"I don't think Captain Baba was thinking about any of those things," said Rufus. "He was thinking about his chances in the afterlife. What if the Catholics are right about religion?"

"You are probably right," I conceded. "The Catholics see themselves as the first, the original and therefore the only authentic Christian denomination. They claim that their popes are descended from Peter the Apostle. I think that belief got to Baba at the last moment."

There was a period of silence. Maas Dan ordered the next round. We moved on to other topics. Later I left to have supper with my family.

When I awoke the following morning, at around six o' clock, I could still hear Baba's drums coming across the hills and valleys. I wondered how his followers had responded to his astonishing conversion. It could have been my imagination, but the drums sounded less confident. But what did I really have to say to Baba? I asked myself. Later that morning our family would be going to our Methodist church. That denomination was founded by an Englishman named John Wesley.

Ancestors

The headmaster's cottage was nestled in a hollow between the hill on which the school was situated and a section of the neighbouring community. From the backyard we had a view of the mountains which formed the backbone of the island. From the front-yard we could see a long ridge dotted with houses below which a winding road followed the folds of its contour. At 7:30 a.m. each weekday I left my study and climbed the hill to the school. As soon as I got to the water tank, I bellowed a problem in arithmetic to the pupils who were waiting in the senior class. By the time I got inside the building I expected the problem to be solved.

Weekends at the cottage were usually quiet. You did not hear the constant hum of children's voices coming from the school. Sometimes you would hear a cow mooing in a nearby pasture. At night, sometimes there was the sound of singing and clapping coming from the nearby Poco church. Our biggest dread was the sound systems on weekends, the noise of which often forced us to cover our heads with our pillows.

It was Saturday evening and I was in my study marking scripts. My wife Shirley was in the kitchen cooking beef soup, and its aroma filled the house. My son Ken had not yet returned from the post office. My daughter Pam was in her room sewing a dress.

"Teacher! Teacher!" I heard a man's voice calling.

I went to the door and saw Mr. Orville Solomon standing in the yard. Maas Solly, as he was known to everyone, was probably in his late forties, had a pointed head, thoughtful eyes, and was wearing a white short-sleeved shirt and brown trousers.

"Good evening Teacher Newman," he said.

"Good evening Mr. Solomon. What can I do for you?"

"I would like to have a word with you, sah," he replied. His manner suggested that it was a confidential matter. So I invited him into the study and offered him a seat. His body rested in the chair, but it was clear that his mind was full of other things. I turned my chair around and sat facing him.

"Teacher, duppy giving me hell!" he declared.

I burst out laughing for I did not believe in ghosts.

"You are laughing, Teacher, but this is a very serious matter. You are an educated man and I am not. I thought you could advise me."

"You don't need a teacher. Perhaps you need an obeahman."

"Obeahman, Teacher? I don't deal with those people."

"So tell me about the ghosts," I said.

"You know I got married and built a little house."

"Yes, I was at your wedding, remember? That was quite a speech you gave. You said you have worked all over the island, Montego Bay, Mandeville, Old Harbour, before returning to your home district and marrying pretty, young Miss Cherry."

"Well, the house is haunted."

"Haunted! Why do you think so?"

"Well, from our honeymoon night we heard the voices of people talking in a strange language. Like dem chatting Latin. Then we heard them throwing stones on the roof. At night we hear the doors opening and shutting, even though we find them closed the following morning. One night I saw the shoelaces coming out of our shoes, but I saw no hands pulling them.

"Then one night as we enter the bedroom I saw a baby lying on the bed. A very young baby that look like a Coolie baby. Then it disappear. I alone see the things. Miss Cherry can hear them but doesn't see them. My mother said I was born with a caul over my eyes, which is why I can see ghosts."

"Have you done anything about it?"

"We throw salt and parched peas on the ground. We make the sign of the cross, but that seems to make it even worse. We thinking of getting a black dog that can see them."

"Perhaps it is a poltergeist," I suggested.

"What is that, Teacher?"

"A spirit that they say throws things about. You have any teenagers living nearby? Some say their sexual energy can cause things like that to happen."

"Our house is fairly isolated, as you know."

"You go to church?"

"Not regularly."

"Talk to a parson. Some of them claim they can exorcise spirits."

Mr. Solomon left, obviously feeling very disappointed, for he expected more from a headteacher.

That night as we lay in bed I mentioned his visit to my wife.

"You should take this matter very seriously," she said. "Something very important could be happening at his house." But I was inclined to be dismissive. Perhaps the heightened sexuality of the honeymoon was the real reason for the poltergeist, I told myself. "You know I don't believe in ghosts," I said. "I regard them as metaphors."

"Metaphors, eh," she replied scornfully. "Wait till one of them box you and you will see!"

"Boxed by a metaphor!" I laughed. "I must try that sentence out with my pupils to see what they make of it!"

Our conversation shifted from the ghosts to Solomon and Miss Cherry. "It is a pity their marriage is off to such a ghostly start," I said. We reminisced about their wedding. Solomon had insisted on an oldtime country wedding like the one his parents had had. There was a booth made of bamboo and coconut thatch with the traditional coconut arch tied with the love knot. Shirley remembered the flowers, especially the June roses. The conversation made us remember our own wedding, and we reached for each other.

One morning a few weeks later, I was teaching my pupils how to parse words when one of them gestured that there was someone at the door. I looked and saw Mr. Solomon. I went to speak with him.

"Teacher, there is a cave under my house! Plenty image in it. Graven image!"

"Graven image, eh," I repeated remembering one of the Ten Commandments, and the alleged impact of the Old Testament on the psyche of my country.

"Yes, Teacher, and I think that is where the duppy dem coming from."

"Interesting. Don't do anything to it. Don't touch or remove anything. I will come and look at it."

That evening after school I rode my bicycle to Solomon's home. It was a small, two-bedroom house on top of a hill, about two hundred yards in from the mainroad. Solomon had built it with the help of a loan from a government agency. In his wedding speech he had explained that he had inherited the land from his parents who, before that, had bought it from a plantation owner.

The two things he loved most about the spot, he had told his audience, was the view of the sea and the sound of the river when it rained. I believed the people of the village to be honest, but I still did not want to leave my bicycle on the road, so I pushed it along the path up to the house. I called Mr. Solomon's name and Miss Cherry, his full-breasted young wife who was about half his age, came to the door. She was wearing a white head-tie, a pink frock, and her eyes seemed strained.

"Good evening, Mrs. Solomon. Is your husband at home?"

"He is down the field working. Let me go and call him." She went to the back of the house and I could hear her hollering.

A few minutes later Mr. Solomon came up the path into the yard. He had a machete in his right hand, and his khaki shirt and pants were sweaty and bush-stained. "Ah glad you come, Teacher," he said. "Come let me show you. Wait, let me get my flashlight." He went into the house and returned with the torch. Then he led the way down into the bushes.

I followed him along the path he had cleared to the entrance to the cave. "The opening is small, as you can see," he said, "but it is much bigger inside. One of my goats got away and I was trying to catch her and she ran right inside there. I probably would not have noticed it otherwise." We arrived at the dark entrance. Mr. Solomon bent down and slipped inside. I followed him.

The beam of the flashlight fell on the stalactites hanging from the roof, and on the stalagmites on the floor that we had to be careful not to trip over. "Look at this image," said Mr. Solomon, shining the beam on a figure which was half man and half bird, which was carved out of the rock of the cave wall. I gasped with that rare archaeological feeling of making contact with the past. Mr. Solomon continued to move the beam round the cavern. There were drawings of turtles, lizards and frogs.

"I think you have found an Arawak shrine!" I said with my excitement rising.

"A what, sah?"

"The Arawaks, or Tainos, were the first inhabitants of the island. They were here before the Spaniards, the Africans, the English, and everybody else. You didn't learn about them in school?"

"I didn't get much schooling."

"The Spaniards invaded them, enslaved them, and killed them for sport. Even though they were kind and hospitable to the Spaniards. They caught the white man's diseases. Before long there wasn't a single one left alive."

"Oh my goodness! I heard about the slavery."

"Well, our enslaved forefathers were brought here from Africa to replace them on the canefields."

"And they worshipped idols?"

"They made images of their gods. Like most people. You probably have some images of Jesus in your house. And the Catholics have statues of Mary in their church-yards."

"You mean not a single one is left?" asked Mr. Solomon.

"Some intermarried with the Maroons in the hills. So some of us probably have their blood in our veins."

"I heard about the Maroons. My grandmother was afraid of them."

"That is another story for another time."

We left the cave for an outside world where the colours now seemed brighter and more intense.

"On Monday morning I will be going to the Ministry on school business," I told Mr. Solomon. "When I am finished I will go up to the university to see if I can have a talk with one of the professors. This looks to me as if it could be a very important discovery."

We began walking up the hill. When we got to the yard Miss Cherry came out of the house carrying a bag.

"Some oranges for you," she said.

"Thank you very much, Miss Cherry," I said taking her gift.

"Say hello to your missis and the children," she continued.

"Will do," I replied. I said goodbye, and with the bag in my left hand, I began pushing the bicycle down the path. I could not ride with the bag, so I walked home.

That evening at supper I told my family about the amazing experience. My wife said very little but looked thoughtful. My son Ken was a fifteen year-old history buff and said he would like to see the site. I promised I would take him to see it. My twelve year-old daughter Pam, who wanted to become a lawyer, was interested in the legal ramifications of Mr. Solomon's discovery. How would it affect his life? she wanted to know. I told her we would just have to wait and see.

That night as we lay in bed, my wife and I discussed the matter some more. She lay beside me, her ample form covered by the white sheet which, during the hot nights was sufficient for us.

"It seems that cave was a sacred place for the Tainos," she observed.

"I think so," I replied.

She continued, "It was for them what our churches are for us. Except that they didn't bring their views of the sacred from Spain, Africa, England. They may have come from South America. Or developed right here. And it wasn't a building. It was the land itself. The earth. They saw the earth, this cave, as a sacred place. You realize that?" She turned to look at me.

"I hadn't thought of that," I said.

"How many of us think of that today?" she asked. "The thousands upon thousands leaving the country, the pollution, the degradation of the land. If we think of the Tainos at all we think of fish and bammy, and of words like 'tobacco' and 'hurricane'. But I think that seeing the land as a sacred place is their greatest lesson for us."

"I think you are right, my love," I said. We went to sleep.

I always dress up when I am going to the Ministry. You have to look very distinguished if you are going to make an impression on those sweating clerks with their glasses of ice-water and towels round their necks. So I put on a white shirt with cuff-links, a navy-blue tie with matching trousers and socks, and my shoes were so shine I could almost see my face in them.

After breakfast at daybreak, I went out into the cool morning, clutching my briefcase, and walked down to the square. One of the privileges of being the headmaster was that I drove in the cab of the village truck. I took my seat beside the driver and we set off for the city.

After a full morning combating the Ministry's bureaucracy, I finally managed to complete most of the school's business. I popped into a nearby restaurant and lunched on curry goat with white rice, green bananas, raw vegetables and my usual soda. Then I took a bus to the university.

The secretary in the Department of History directed me to one Dr. Richard Anderson. I followed her directions and found the block, and went up the steps and began following the numbers of the offices. The door of Dr. Anderson's chair-lined office was open, and he was sitting at his desk reading. He had brown hair and his sky-blue shirt was rolled up to his elbows.

"Dr. Anderson?" I said, and he looked up and studied me with his blue eyes.

"Please come in," he said. "Have a seat." I sat on one of the green chairs, and then introduced myself and explained my mission. "What!" he exclaimed. "A Taino site? There are some three hundred of them on the island, but I have never heard of this one." He had a British accent and seemed very enthusiastic about his subject. He opened his diary and we began arranging a date and time for his visit. He wrote down the directions I gave him. "When you get to the square just ask for Mr. Orville Solomon's home," I told him.

"Will do! Will do!" he said. We shook hands and I began walking towards the bus stop.

On the Saturday morning that we had agreed on, my son and I set off on our walk to Mr. Solomon's home. Dr. Anderson had said he would be there at 10:00 a.m., and from my experience with Britons I knew that he meant it, and that it would not be Jamaica Time. It always amazed me that they could travel to virtually anywhere on the island, and in spite of the bad roads and traffic, still arrive on the stroke of the agreed hour.

We arrived at the home of the Solomons and stood in the yard chatting while we awaited the arrival of the scholar. Miss Cherry was quite fascinated by Ken, and kept expressing her amazement at how much he had grown. Mr. Solomon and I chatted about the cave. I had read up on the Tainos and had a few more bits of information to offer him.

"Dem coming," said Mr. Solomon at 9:50 a.m. I looked and saw Dr. Anderson coming up the path. I wondered if Mr. Solomon's "dem" was a plural in the Jamaican language I wasn't aware of. Dr. Anderson was wearing a checkered shirt, jeans, and what looked like white hiking shoes. He had a knapsack on his back. "Welcome, Dr. Anderson," I said as he entered the yard. I made the introductions.

"Where is the other man?" asked Mr. Solomon.

"I am alone," replied the historian, looking puzzled.

"There was another man walking behind you," insisted Mr. Solomon. Dr. Anderson and I looked at each other. The scholar's eyes seemed to be questioning Solomon's integrity and reliability.

"What did he look like?" I asked Mr. Solomon.

"He was wearing no shirt. Had long, black hair."

"Sounds like a Taino," I said. "The Solomons have been experiencing ghosts," I explained to Dr. Anderson. I had neglected this bit of information when I spoke to him in his office.

"Ghosts!" he exclaimed. "I don't know anything about ghosts!"

"Are you still seeing and hearing them?" I asked Mr. Solomon.

"Not since we heard that Dr. Anderson was coming," he replied. "And just now."

"Their spirits are probably now pacified," I said. "Let's go look at the cave."

At the entrance to the cave Dr. Anderson opened his knapsack and took out a flashlight-helmet and put it on his head. He also took out a camera and began taking photographs of the site. Solomon entered the cave and Ken and I followed him.

"Holy Moses!" exclaimed Dr. Anderson as soon as he saw the artefacts. "This is the best site I have ever seen!"

The flash of his camera kept lighting up the cavern as he recorded whatever he saw that was of interest to him.

"Our archaeologist is off the island at the moment attending a conference in Australia, but I will bring him here as soon as he gets back. To preserve the integrity of the site let's keep it a secret until the experts have had a chance to study it. We need to document it carefully before we go to the newspapers. We don't want crowds descending on the place and destroying it. You heard me Mr. Solomon?"

"Yes sah. Is only me, Miss Cherry and Teacher know about it. I don't want the people in the area to think is obeah I working down here!"

I laughed at his response to the so-called 'pagan' Tainos.

When Dr. Anderson was satisfied we went outside into the sunshine.

"I will get you some water coconuts," said Mr. Solomon as he began walking towards a nearby tree. We watched as he climbed the trunk with great strength and skill. During his wedding speech he had told us about his many jobs: as a fisherman in Old Harbour Bay, a fruit vendor in Porus, a welder in Kingston.

But I felt he was probably best at the skills he had honed right there in his district. He began throwing down coconuts, skillfully aiming them at spots in the bushes where they would not roll away. Then he slithered down the trunk and began opening the fruits, cutting holes at the tips for us to drink from, and cutting off little strips to be used as spoons. We satisfied our thirst, and then sat in the grass and began chatting.

"Mr. Solomon, you built your house over a cave," observed Ken. "What happen if there is an earthquake?"

"To tell you the truth I have thought about it," replied Solomon.

"It looks like mostly rock," said Dr. Anderson. "It would take a very powerful quake to make the house fall in."

"So what are you going to do, Dr. Anderson?" I asked.

"As academics, our job is to study it first to see what it can add to our store of knowledge. The rest will be up to the government."

"The government!" said Mr. Solomon with alarm.

"I am going to make some recommendations," continued Dr. Anderson. "First of all they will definitely want to make it into a heritage site. I think they should employ Mr. Solomon as the guide."

"Me?" objected Mr. Solomon. "I don't have any education."

"They could train you," I suggested.

"And they should name the cave after you," continued Dr. Anderson.

"They should name it after the goat!" said Mr. Solomon. "It was she who found it."

"'Solomon's Cave' sounds better than 'Goat Cave'," I said with a laugh.

"I am writing a book on the Tainos," said Dr. Anderson, "and this cave and Mr. Solomon will figure very prominently in it."

"Me in a book?" said Mr. Solomon as if having difficulty adjusting to all these new responsibilities. It seemed to me that he only wanted to settle down and raise a family.

"You going to be famous, Mr. Solomon," said Ken. "Children will read about you in school."

"I spent less than a year in school," said Mr. Solomon.

"So Dr. Anderson," I said, "how did you become interested in the Tainos?"

"I have some American ancestry, and I am part Cherokee."

"Really! You don't look it," I said.

"It is buried deep, but it is there. I think it is the root of my interest in the history of New World peoples."

"I believe heritage should be for the people first," I said. "But this development could also mean something for tourism and the economic development of this community."

"Definitely," said Dr. Anderson.

"Mr. Solomon, you have everything going for this museum. You even have your own ghost!" I said.

"If we respect him, he probably won't mash up the place," said Mr. Solomon.

Our discussion over, it was time to make our way back to the yard. Mr. Solomon offered Dr. Anderson some coconuts to take home with him, and he accepted gratefully, saying water coconuts were one of the main delights of the island.

We walked up the hill carrying coconuts for Miss Cherry, and some for Dr. Anderson's car. We spent a few minutes chatting in the yard, then said goodbye to Miss Cherry and headed for the road. Dr. Anderson thanked Mr. Solomon for the coconuts and shook hands with us. We agreed to keep in touch and work together towards the development of the project. Then he drove away.

Ken and I began walking home. Ken was now speaking excitedly about the things he had seen and heard. I listened in silence, while reflecting on the bed-talk with my wife about sacred places. And on the fact that this district of Yaville will never be the same again.